Sign up at pgshriver.com now to receive news of
new releases and special offers.

I0730854

Note to Readers

This book is a work of fiction and in no way offers suggestions or guidance on dealing with an abuser. If you or a loved one is seeking a way out of an abusive relationship, please contact the National Domestic Violence Hotline at 800-799-7233.

We all deserve to be happy and lead fulfilling lives. Abuse is not about happiness. It's about power.

By the Way...

P. G. SHRIVER

Acknowledgements

I would like to thank my beta readers for their thoughts and time. I would also like to thank my fans who have waited for so long for a new release.

I would also like to acknowledge the Family Abuse Centers of America for their unrelenting help and desire to correct an ongoing problem in relationships throughout the United States. Without FAC's men, women and children would have no place to escape the horrible truths that hide behind closed doors. FAC's truly give meaning to "the pursuit of happiness" in this country—a happiness each of us deserves.

Dedication

This book is dedicated to the ladies in my life:
Mikayla
Miranda
Dawn
Esther
Casie
Lisa
And all the girls in our family coming into relationships
of their own.

The bicycle tire spun into my view, silver spokes a blur in my peripheral vision.

As my horn sounded, I remember comparing the tire to those on the bikes Matt and I rode around campus when we were in college.

The thought of Matt made me smile just before my foot stomped the brake pedal.

It was because of Matt that I was running late.

The screech from my tires brought neighbors to their front doors, out onto their crisp, frost capped winter lawns. Steam roiled from coffee cups, drifting upward to conceal the shocked faces of each flannel-robe-wearing neighbor.

The time between the appearance of the tire and the roiling coffee steam felt like years as the scene played out in slow motion.

Matt and I once lived in a neighborhood similar to

this one, I recalled as my rear tires fishtailed on the damp road before jarring to a stop.

My coffee rested in the cup holder near the gearshift and never moved. I glanced at it and wished it was in my hand while I stood on a lawn next to Matt staring blankly at the accident in front of our house.

My left temple plunked onto the top of the steering wheel. I was afraid to look up, afraid to get out of the car, afraid to see the person lying in the road in front of my SUV.

Frozen in time and space, an icy crystal joining the others on the grass beyond the window, I kept my thoughts on Matt as people hovered, gathered, peered inside at me with their hands, shielding their eyes as if to better see through the tinted glass.

Large, white knuckles rapped three times on the driver side window. A male voice, gruff and raspy, drifted into my muffled world, "Are you okay? Can you move? An ambulance is coming. Just stay put. Stay right there."

Through the windshield, I saw a silver haired woman duck down at the front of my car's hood.

A whoosh of cold air introduced a soft hand, warm and wrinkled, its fingertips coated with pink polish as it reached in from the passenger side door and pushed the start button to kill the murmuring engine. I glanced questioningly toward her face; chipper blue eyes crinkled with sympathy, "Everything's fine. Just stay right here." The kind woman patted my arm gently, sympathetically, then retracted her arm and closed the door; the chilly breeze filled the cabin, brushed my cheek, and left behind one warm spot where Matt's lips connected earlier that morning whispering words of passion.

People moved, hovered, fluttered in slow motion in and out of my limited vision.

Shock settled in and I shivered. I felt myself slipping away.

Matt could not overpower the coming realization of what I had done. As sirens wailed in the distance, my world stopped.

I hit a person.

I hit a person on a bicycle.

At one time, that might have been me.

It might have been Matt.

What if it was a child on his way to school? Was school in session now?

My thoughts jumbled and wandered as I squeezed my eyelids together and the tears came. I was afraid to look up, afraid I might see the cyclist twisted and mangled on the road. Replaying the incident, I searched my memories for a face, but mental stubbornness only revealed the tire.

I had taken my eyes off the road for just a second... one second.

I opened and shut my eyes, resting my forehead on the padded steering wheel.

The tire spun into my view again, and my imagination revealed images of numerous body parts lying in the road, mutilated by one tap from my speeding vehicle. I opened my eyes to stop the images and stared at my dashboard. I tried to think of Matt, but my vision tunneled, darkness slowly closing around a tiny circle of focus on my dashboard—84 miles to E.

My driver's door opened flooding me with another rush of brisk air, an icy front pushing away the warm rush of summer produced by my overactive imagination.

A thick, comforting blanket draped over my shoulders.

Firm hands rubbed gently, up and down, on my jacket-clad arms, my sleeves creating useless warmth beneath; the friction dominated by numbness.

"You're going to be okay. Try to take some deep breaths." The man's voice sounded as if he were at the other end of a tunnel whispering to me. The siren in the background stopped.

I looked to the carpeted floor at my feet, my cell phone resting face up just below the brake pedal, a text bubble of my unsent message, "BTW… I love you."

Darkness hovered, circled, crept over the message.

"Where are you taking me?" The excitement overwhelmed me. I was not a patient woman, and Matt knew it.

"Just keep your eyes closed. We're almost there." I leaned into the arm rest so I didn't lose my balance as Matt made a left turn. He drove a little farther from where we made the turn, then stopped. "Just a little longer. Take off your seat belt, but don't look." Matt said before I heard his car door open.

Memories of all the romantic events we'd shared played through my mind. What was he up to now? I thought.

My car door opened and I felt Matt's hand on my elbow lifting me up out of the car just like that first day in college.

"Now?" I asked impatiently. I was shaking with anticipation.

His hand traveled to my waist before he squeezed me into his side. "Now." He said the word so quietly I almost didn't hear it.

My eyes opened to a beautiful, modern home with large windows and wide open spaces. The lawn was well manicured. A large oak stood at the front near the sidewalk. A private fence branched out from one side of the house and the garage.

"I don't get it. Are we staying here tonight? I mean, this looks like somebody's house." I wrinkled my nose at him in question. There had to be more to this adventure.

"It is somebody's house."

"Well, it looks empty Matt. Is it one of those AirBnB homes or something?" I stepped sideways to look up at him.

"Or something." He smiled down at me.

"Matt— what's going on? Do you have some romantic night planned in this house? What is it? You've never delayed surprising me like this. Picking me up from work… having lunch… driving me way out here? We're already engaged so…" He took my hand and led me up the stone walkway toward the front door.

The door opened to an empty house. Now I was really confused.

After trailing him through the entire downstairs, we stopped in the dining area divided from the patio and back yard with multiple floor to ceiling windows offering a view of an in ground pool and spa, a beautiful garden with a blue stone pathway, and another large oak with a wooden swing hanging from it.

"Oh my god, Matt! This yard… this house… it's perfect." At which point he guided me away to the upstairs. After leading me down a short hallway, through the master bathroom with its low rise stone shower guarded by a half wall to the right of the entrance—a rainwater shower head hanging from the center—a deep antique, claw foot tub, and a delicate, built-in vanity just beyond the shower, Matt paused in front of a closed door. I stuttered before asking, "Why is the AirBnB empty? This has to be the most elegant place we've stayed in."

"It's not an AirBnB." Matt faced me his smile playful and curious as he as he pushed down on the door lever and swung open the door behind him. He kept his eyes on my face and as it changed to awe, he said, "Welcome to our new bedroom."

Left speechless by his comment, I scanned the room lighted only by the brilliance of the six floor to ceiling windows, intricately etched glass reflecting a romantic glow across the walls. The only items in the room had been placed strategically upon the multi shaded grey hardwood floor: a mattress, a bucket of chilled champagne, two champagne flutes, a box of chocolate covered strawberries, and a board of sliced cheeses.

"W… W… What?!" I asked as I slipped past him into the large space. Skirting the mattress, I took in the view from every window. The neighbors were just far enough away to allow for privacy behind a tree and shrub lined property border. It wasn't anything like our cozy apartment.

"How? When?" I spun to face him. "Matt?"

"You love it, right?" Matt moved toward me, took me in his arms and smiled down at me.

"Well, I love you…" I teased, tracing his lips with my index finger.

"You don't love the house?" He pulled back and frowned.

"Of course I love it!" My voice raised excitedly as I jumped up and down. "It has everything we've ever talked about having. Matt, when did you buy this house?"

"Remember that day I didn't drive you to work?" He raised his brows. I nodded. "I was at the closing."

"Oh, Matt!" I pressed my lips to his.

"Let's take advantage of our first night in our new home… alone. The movers will be here in the morning." He returned my kiss, the heat between us rising to uninhibited passion.

We woke up the next morning to a knock on the front door, clothes scattered around the floor, an empty champagne bottle floating in a bucket of water, and an empty chocolate box sitting atop the cheese board.

My eyes fluttered, opening to a different world.

Specks of popcorn texturing, tiny rises and shadows on my bedroom ceiling, became more visible with each blink.

The fuzziness cleared from my sleepy eyes as my hand found the cold pillow next to me, the bed sheets below the pillow smooth and tight. The dawning light intensified as the earth moved forward on its daily journey, its brilliant light streaking through the blinds to brighten the opposite wall.

I didn't want to move.

I didn't want to start the day.

I wanted Matt. I needed his warmth, the safe feeling he provided, the security I felt lying next to him.

Matt was no longer here.

He hadn't been here in…

How long had it been? I asked myself. Tears stung my eyes and I fought to choke them back as I remembered the last night I'd shared with Matt, the last night he'd been attentive, gentle, loving—the night before...

I closed my eyes against the horrible memory.

After that night, our love died— well, his love died. Mine lingered on and each morning after waking from the nightmare, I searched for him.

Several times a day, I dialed his number, touching the small x seven times to delete it immediately afterward. He wouldn't take the call, anyway. He'd had enough the day he walked away, and that was—how long ago?

At times I felt him, still here with me; I almost couldn't tell the difference our last days so resembled my current lonely state, but he wasn't here. He'd left me alone to sink into the darkness— a darkness of my own creation. He was tired of waiting, longing for the love he remembered, the love I could no longer give him. He deserved better. I understood that.

He had to go.

Besides, nobody should have to wait forever.

At times, my mind tricked me into believing our life together had been a fantasy, none of it real, just a love I'd created through all the craziness post accident. Matt became a man from the pages of a romance novel I'd read sometime in my past. God knows he resembled every one of them in some way or another.

At other times, I wanted to believe my entire life thus far had been a dream, that one day I would wake up and see that all of it had been just some illusion, some trick of the lens.

And sometimes, I clung to that idea just so I could rise each morning and continue to live.

My doctor would not approve of my "illusion" world, but when the spokes rolled in from my past, that was the only way I could cope.

I missed Matt so much, and I only had myself to blame.

If only...

"Andi, come on! We're going to be late!" Matt's deep, raspy warning carried down the hallway into the bedroom.

"Well, whose fault is that? I was ready an hour ago!" I smiled and shook my head at his urgency as I tugged at the zipper of my black knee high boot. One down, one to go.

"Uh, huh. I didn't care much for the outfit you had on. It looked better on the floor," Matt teased. "I'm gonna warm up the car."

I heard the kitchen door to the garage close as I pulled on my leather coat and grabbed my Coach handbag off the hook. Glancing at the clock on the stove, I grimaced and slipped out the kitchen door locking it behind me—8:15, yes, I was going to be late for work… again. I moved swiftly to the passenger side of the sedan. Matt reached across the seat and pushed the door open for me.

"Hmm, you're glowing… all pink and happy. Everybody's gonna *know* why you're late…"

"I'm not!" I pulled the visor down and flipped the mirror cover upward. *Oh, crap!*

Matt slid his hand under my hair, turned my face to him and pulled me into a passionate kiss. "Have I told you lately that you're beautiful?" He asked as I pushed away from him. "We have to go!" Wide eyed, I placed my left hand on the side of his face as if to caress his cheek, then turned his face toward the windshield.

The garage door slid open as he placed his arm on the back of the seat and turned to look over his shoulder. "You know this car has a backup camera." I made fun of his refusal to use the feature.

"Never needed one before." Having reached the end of the driveway, he paused to be sure the garage door closed before he turned his twinkling eyes toward me suggesting a sick day as he raised his brows.

"No! You have that big presentation today. I have an article to finish. We have to go in!" He pulled me into another passionate kiss before glancing both ways and behind him, again. "Your lipstick is kind of smeared." He winked at me.

I pulled the visor down again, opened the mirror, and reached into my bag for a tissue.

Matt was always such a careful driver. I admired

that about him. The entire time we dated, he was so cautious. His driving record reflected it, too. As he pulled out into the frosty street, his cell phone buzzed in his briefcase. The navigation screen showed the number. He pushed the red 'off' signal and let it go to voicemail.

"You could have answered that. This car does everything," I reminded him, knowing it was the bank that he'd hung up on just then.

"This car does not drive itself. Nor does it keep you and I and the rest of the world safe while I drive it. That call will wait until I get to work. You're not gonna catch me putting on my lipstick while I'm driving." He smiled out the front windshield; that last bit comment directed at me.

His strong profile against the background of the neighborhood houses as each whizzed by at thirty miles an hour sent me dreaming; I couldn't help but smile. I loved this man so much. I reached my hand out and pushed a strand of his dark chin length hair behind his ear, its waviness escaping from the rest. He never even glanced my way. No distractions while driving, that was his rule. A flush from my cheeks sent electrical shivers down the back of my neck and into my arms as I watched him, so calm, confident and… well, for lack of a better word, gorgeous. How had I gotten so lucky to have met him in college?

"You're staring at me. If you keep it up, I'll turn around and go home." His eyes cut a sideways glance my way, a playful half smile lighting his face as he turned his attention back to the road.

"Okay, you caught me." I faced the street in front of us and noted the ice tipped grass on either side from the frost early that morning. By ten it would be gone, but for the ride to work now, it gave our drive a magical feel. Matt reached for my hand, brought it to his lips where he kissed my knuckles lightly, then rested them on his heart. "No distractions," I reminded.

"I'm not distracted. I'm in love." His eyes never left the road as my hand, pressed into his chest, felt the warmth beneath the light blue dress shirt, the steady thump of his heart.

Later that morning, I went to the lounge for a cup of coffee. The frost had cleared away from the third floor window, I watched steam roll in the chilly air above the power plant miles away. My phone vibrated as I sipped the hot caramel flavored liquid. I thumbed the home button and tapped the message icon. It was from Matt.

BTW… I love you.

That was our signal. It meant that by two o'clock that afternoon, we would be back home and in bed. The power couple with a powerful love and incredible desire for each other.

Our life was perfect.

A horse whinnied beyond my bedroom window, my call to rise and shine. A tormented sigh escaped my lips.

Get up, I scolded myself. Start your day. Make the coffee. Take care of the farm. It was the only way to keep the darkness from swallowing me, bit by bit, forcing me forever into an abyss of depression and rage.

Rolling to face the empty side of my bed, I allowed one last caress of the cold pillow, one last memory of a late passionate morning, the love Matt and I shared, the feel of his thick, dark hair, tousled from a night's sleep, his lips against mine, his breath caressing my neck.

In bittersweet frustration, I rolled away, threw back the comforter, and forced myself out of bed. The cold hardwood floor brought a chill up my legs as I moved across it to my bathroom and closet.

Work waited for me beyond the house. I lived on this farm alone and my animals depended on my sanity.

I didn't have time for memories of Matt. It was useless to relive our past life together or imagine him living this life with me. "The present is all that matters," I repeated aloud the phrase my therapist told me to repeat when the past took control of my thoughts. "I live today."

I would never see Matt again and I had to accept that, embrace the change, muster my strength, get on with life and all those other platitudes sympathetic people offered each other. Did they know how difficult it was to live up to those platitudes?

The coffee maker percolated as I yawned, stretched, and glared at a pink Post-it note staring back at me from the freezer door.

Man coming for Winks 10/1~ 2 pm

Today? Today was 10/1! Crap! My finger moved lightly over the taped strip along the top, caressing the note as a melancholy settled in my heart. I had forgotten a potential buyer was coming to ride Winks. The phone number drew my interest briefly. I thought about calling the buyer, telling him I was too busy today. The truth was I really didn't want to have a long, drawn-out meeting with some jerk about a horse, and he had been a jerk when he called— a wealthy jerk.

If not for the fact that I had a balloon payment due on the farm, I would call and cancel. But the buyer had the money to back his rude behavior as well as a spoiled daughter to spend his money on.

I loved Winks. Of all the horses I'd raised and trained, he was my favorite. Selling him would be difficult. I wasn't looking forward to haggling over a price with the man who called, either. Tapping the post it, I resolved to stick to my price; maybe the buyer would give up and go away, but then I would have to find another way to make my payment.

Coffee creamer in hand, I opened the cabinet door and reached for a mug, poured a little creamer in the bottom and placed it back in the fridge. The coffee pot gurgled its final notice of completion, so I pulled it from the warmer and watched the hot dark liquid swirl the cream in as the coffee filled my mug.

A chill hung in the air when I stepped out onto the porch, the horizon hiding the bottom half of the sun. There was still time for the morning show. The wooden rocker felt cold beneath my flannel pajama bottoms briefly scolding me for not slipping my robe on or changing into the clothes I had lain out on the bed before taking coffee to the porch. Yes—I agreed patting the rocker arm—I probably should have put on a robe at least. Sipping my coffee, I watched the new foals stretching as they faced the rising sun. Most of the mares stood facing the sun every morning, one or two grazed. My favorite times were dawn and dusk when the foals tested their muscles, running through the pasture.

Winks had been one of those foals a few years ago. I grinned at his past mischief.

Now he was ready to leave the farm. He stood at the fence, head draped over the top board, watching the foals bounce and buck. I knew what he would do, and waited patiently for his show.

He could never resist.

Oh, how I would regret selling him. His personality was one of a kind. His beautiful fawn colored coat, with his dark mane, tail, and markings stood out in the rising sunlight. The tips of Winks' mane lifted and curled upward in the breeze. Just a wisp of white lined his strong, straight nose that mildly dipped just above his nostrils. I smiled when he glanced my way, eye contact seeming to ask, "Are you ready?"

Sipping slowly as the sun crept upward through lines of distant dark clouds, the foals began their dance and Winks, as usual, left the fence line at a gallop and circled out into his pasture, tail held high. He turned to face the fence that joined the foals' pasture. From a gallop, he stretched his front legs forward, pushed off the ground with his hind legs, and gracefully left a good three inches between his belly and the top board of the fence, landing right in the midst of the playful foals. A younger foal crossed before him, just as his forelegs touched the ground, bringing him to a pause in a momentary horsey hand stand, and then off he ran, bucking, kicking, tossing his head like a big old baby.

Winks' near miss with the young foal brought the bicycle tire to my mind, but I quickly pushed it into the dark recesses refusing to let it grab hold as it did in my sleep. My attention returned to the foals, some of the mares— the younger ones— joining in the fun, snorting and nickering at Winks, rising to his raring challenge as his forelegs scraped the air above them. *He's so beautiful. I should raise my price*, I thought.

One more cup of coffee, then I need to get dressed, get to work in the barn, I told myself.

I returned to the kitchen, refilled my mug and carried the newly steaming cup back to the porch. By the time my mug was emptied, Winks was back in his own pasture nickering at me, curling his top lip upward to show his large teeth in a horsy smile. "I made you smile," he seemed to say.

The little devil.

The first time Winks jumped the fence, I chased him around all morning trying to get him back in the yearlings' pasture. When I finally gave up and resorted to call help from down the road, he jumped back into his own pasture. He'd been doing that for two years now, every morning, never once catching that top board or hurting a foal. Some horses were just meant to jump. The man coming to look at him wanted him for that very reason.

The bicycle tire rotated into view, again.

Why was the memory of my accident haunting me so much today? Usually I could push it back, let it go and focus on the day. Today, it forced itself back into every moment.

"You're lucky!" Coworkers told me. I didn't feel lucky. Just because the person hadn't died didn't mean I was lucky. I knew they were referring to the lack of manslaughter charges. There hadn't been any criminal charges and there were none pending, but then, the accident had happened before the law on texting while driving went into effect.

Still, the damage was done, physically and mentally. I would have to live with the guilt of that mistake for the rest of my life— a prison enough, I guess, one built by self judgement.

No, I didn't consider myself lucky at all.

After the accident, I started freelancing from home. I couldn't return everyday to those sympathetic stares and curious minds. The horse farm brought in enough money for me to live on. The freelancing was extra. Through the years following, I'd become a hermit, staying on my farm as much as possible, driving less and less. When I did drive, I had to block the memory, and I drove like a granny on Sunday, my hands never leaving the wheel, my eyes never straying from the road.

Today, for the first time in a while, I had awakened and reached out for the pillow beside me, for Matt.

Why had I done that?

"Well, *you* hit somebody while texting and try to go back to your normal life," I argued back at him.

"You've changed, Andi. I can't do this anymore, live like this. You're just not…"

"Myself?" I finished Matt's statement. "My, God, Matt! I almost killed somebody texting *you* while I was driving! What do you want me to be like?"

"It's not me, Andi! It's not my fault. You can't blame *me* for that, but somehow I feel like you are blaming me, or at least blaming our love for each other."

"But it was *our* thing, wasn't it? It was…"

"I'm not going to say it, Andi. You tell yourself that all you want, but I won't rip us apart with those four words. I love you. I want you back, like you were before…"

I wiped a tear from my eye and blinked against his words. How could I be the woman I was before the accident? How could I go back and not let this accident come between us?

"I don't know, Matt. I don't know how to be that person anymore."

"Then let's get you some help to cope. I want you back. Please come back to me."

The tears fell freely as I turned away and pushed the curtains aside. The backyard lay in a blanket of darkness. I'd had another nightmare about the accident and Matt woke up to find me curled up in the chair quivering. Now I felt the exterior darkness seeping through the window, reaching for me, and I wanted it to swallow me up in its depths. The very windows I'd found comfort in and inspiration through all those years now attacked me with my own reflection of guilt.

I felt Matt's strong fingers grip my shoulders, rubbing lightly. I looked up at his sad eyes above my reflection before he turned me away from the window to face him. His fingertips gently tipped my chin up as he searched my eyes. "We can get through this, Andi. It was an accident." He'd reassured me.

"I don't know how." I replied just before streams of hot tears flowed down my cheeks and Matt pulled me into his chest, his strong shoulder dampened with my crazy tears.

The accident, the nightmares, the breakup, all led to my melt down.

A delayed nervous breakdown, my doctors called it. At times, when I dwelled on the past, I believed it hadn't been real at all, that none of it was real—not even Matt. I'd always thought he was too good to be true, that we had the perfect life, the perfect love.

Reality wasn't perfect.

I told myself it was all fantasy— a dumb, romantic, tragic fantasy created by years of working for a romance magazine; it was, wasn't it? I convinced myself it was a fantasy because the reality of believing it happened and ended was too painful. My self loathing imprisonment was worse than any consequences I could have faced if I'd been arrested.

I felt myself slipping into that depressing breakdown darkness, for one tiny second, before I snapped my head up and returned my attention to Winks.

This was my reality, my sanity, my courage. My animals didn't know how much they helped me cope, or did they? A chuckle escaped my throat after I reached for my empty coffee mug receiving a handful of fur in return, black fur that I instantly started to scratch, "Good morning, Mac." The cat purred from deep within the mug as she lapped up the remnants of cream filled coffee. She loved coffee— well, the cream filled coffee, no sugar, no plain. Once Mac had her fill from the bottom of my cup, I picked up the mug. Her satisfied smile grew as she licked her paws and washed her face. Every last drop of creamy coffee had disappeared. I stroked her head, "I can't sit here all day, girl."

The old Ford tractor waited in front of the barn, ready for me to repair the fuel line this morning. I had to finish seeding the backfield with rye tomorrow. The horses would need winter grass before long. The more I thought about everything I needed to do before my two o'clock meeting, the more my heart quickened and the faster the memories entered and faded from my thoughts.

What was the deal?

Why was I wasting so much time on the misery of my past today?

Self-deprecating anger built within before I stormed into the house, old feelings bringing a tremble, old actions taking over. Leaving the coffee maker on and opting for no breakfast, I returned to my room to dress for the day. Anything to keep my mind busy.

I could feel myself beginning to sink each time I

paused to think.

No more days in bed; No more dwelling on the past; all that matters is today, I repeated.

Mother had been a believer in signs and her voice swirled through the memories telling me to check with the hospital, something must have happened… maybe it was good news. Your thoughts, your actions, the dreams, they're all signs, Mother's silent words coaxed.

Maybe I should check, I told myself as I paused near my bed where my clothes lay in wait.

Lifting the worn jeans from the bed, I swapped out my pajama bottoms. My long sleeve denim shirt I shrugged into next, then—second sock tugged on—instead of reaching for my boots near my nightstand, I reached for my cell phone laying on top of it. I couldn't count the failed attempts, the numerous times I dialed six of the seven numbers for the hospital. Again, I started to dial, touched seven numbers, one ring and I hung up. I couldn't know, didn't want to hear the nurse tell me there was a change for the worst, that the person in question had died.

I didn't want to hear that.

I had to let it go.

Thirty minutes later, I was outside, the crisp fresh air filling my lungs with each focused controlled breath. The distance to the barn grew shorter with my steps and the horses, hearing the feed room door slide open, gathered at their respective troughs.

Feeding complete, I went to the shop to locate the tools and open the box of parts for the tractor while the horses ate; I grabbed an empty bucket and filled it with everything I needed. I loathed mechanic work. I couldn't stand the grease and oil sticking to my skin, under my nails, but paying somebody else for a task this simple was an unaffordable luxury. Besides, it kept my mind busy researching, learning, and doing— anything to remain sane. Thank goodness for the Internet, Youtube and Google.

I would start on the tractor after I'd exercised all of the horses, so I left the bucket of tools on the tractor seat to help warm up the fuel line and tools. The horses were my livelihood. They always came first.

The prep work for the tractor finished, I went into the barn and waited for the young girl who lived next door to show up. She couldn't afford a horse of her own, but she was a natural with them. I'd made a deal with her mother for Rachel to work off the purchase of one of the three year olds. Of course, he wouldn't be three when she finally took him home. Rachel came over every morning to help me, and to have her riding lessons— free of charge. Doing good for others slightly relieved my guilt over the accident.

Rachel's curly blonde ponytail bounced as she ran across the pasture between our houses, leaping over broom grass, small mesquites, and fallen tree branches like a gazelle in flight. The pasture between us belonged to her parents. One of Rachel's chores was to clean it up so they'd have a place for Trooper when she finally got to bring him home. I grinned and waved after she jumped down from the top rail of the horse fence. Her enthusiastic smile reminded me of myself when I was her age. Maybe that's another reason I agreed to the deal. I had a wonderful childhood, with all the ponies and horses I wanted.

"Hey, Andi!" She waved.

"Good morning! Ready to jump today?" I put on a sincere look and pursed my lips.

"Really?" Her eyes widened. This was the day she'd been waiting for since the first time she'd laid eyes on Trooper.

"Yeah, I think you're ready," I assured her, smiling this time.

"Wow!" She jumped up and down a few times spinning a circle, then ran to the barn to get Trooper ready for the lesson.

"You know, I was thinking, next spring, you might be ready for a show. Do you think your parents would let you ride along with me?" The ulterior motive for getting her in the ring was marketing. I couldn't ride and network with the riders' parents. Then there was the drive… I'd avoided driving to shows and had been using online ads to bring in business. To say the least, that hadn't worked as well as I'd hoped. My ranch was accumulating more horses than sales.

"Oh my gosh! Are you serious?" Rachel turned back toward me and threw her arms around my neck, hugging me tightly. "I'll make them let me! Oh, wow! I can't believe it!" She grabbed Trooper's halter and rope and I watched as he met her in the pasture. Those two were made for each other.

Why can't relationships between people be that way? Meet me halfway. Understand me just a little. I believed Matt and I were like that once… seeing each other every time like it was our first time.

Leaving Trooper tied with the other three year olds, Rachel quickly mucked out the stalls, then lunged

Trooper in the round pen, warming his muscles as she did every morning. She'd ride him while I rode whatever horse I worked, then in late morning she'd return home to do her school work. Rachel's mother, an ex teacher, had homeschooled her since Rachel was three. I seated myself on Winks, my last ride on him before his visitor— and potential new owner— arrived at two. I knew in my heart Winks would be leaving the ranch today. There was probably a young girl, just like Rachel, at home that the buyer wanted to surprise with the perfect jumper. I patted Winks' strong neck, rubbed lightly up and down. Winks needed a little girl like Rachel, somebody with enthusiasm and youth, somebody who would play with him, love him, be his person for life.

Rachel and Trooper now stood at the entrance to the arena; Rachel searched my face across the distance for my nod. "You're ready! Go on, run the pattern and this time, take the jumps. Keep your internal excitement to a minimum. You've been preparing for this. Ride it like you've ridden it a hundred times!" I nodded at her. And she did run it like she'd done it all of her life. Perfect seat, perfect balance, perfect jumps, perfect run —a natural. Winks couldn't keep still as Trooper breezed through the pattern. He wanted to be out there and his hooves stomped in expectation. "You'll get your turn. Be patient, Winks." I stroked his neck.

After we finished exercising and working with the few three year olds on the schedule, the yearlings were next, and then Rachel started home, her wiry frame disappearing through the shrubbery. I shook my head as she stopped, bent down to pick up a piece of tree limb, then changed her mind and kicked it instead. Her mother's voice carried through the cool breeze, calling the young girl to her schoolwork.

I began the tedious work of mechanics. I wished I could find a young man who needed a horse and was interested in tractors. I would gladly trade another horse for upkeep on tractors and equipment. The fuel line that required replacement wasn't going to be an easy task, especially on this old of a tractor. First of all, it was nearly impossible to reach. But for my slender hands, long fingers and strength from typing, I may not have gotten it apart. Leaning into the tractor, loose tendrils of golden brown hair falling about my face, full concentration on getting the new line in place, I missed the sound of a motor, the crunch of tires on gravel, the closing of a heavy truck door. I didn't even hear my Pyrenees barking, though it was her that alerted me to the visitor when she escorted him toward the barn; her large feet landed in the middle of my back while I reached into the small opening on the tractor engine and pushed the fuel line in place.

"Ouch!" I pulled away from the tractor and glanced over my shoulder. "Why on earth did you do that? Can't you see I'm busy, Reba?" She moved out of view, tail wagging, a satisfied smile on her face, event though I turned my head to issue a scolding look at her as she rounded the tractor. I bit off the words of warning for my dog when I came face to face with a man standing across from me. His hand dangled at his side, fingers delicately scratching behind my dog's ears. "Oh, I'm sorry. I didn't know you were there." My mood quickly changed to one of welcome. His gaze moved downward toward Reba then back up, providing him opportunity to scan my face before our eyes met. A hint of curious humor crinkled the corners of his eyes, as if it were his first time to see a female mechanic.

Grabbing the grease rag on the tractor seat, I wiped gooey, slippery, sticky grease from my hands, generously squirted some hand cleaner from the orange jug into my palm, rubbed it around and wiped my hands with a clean rag. They were clean. That orange stuff was amazing, and it smelled good, too.

"I'm looking for Andy. Andy… " he pulled a post it note from his shirt pocket, "Melton? Is he here?"

A close mouthed chuckle and shake of my head confused him. I loved the fact that everyone who emailed me thought I was a guy. It never ceased to make me laugh when they realized their error.

"That," I stuck my hand out, "would be me. Andrianna Melton. Andi for short… with an i." I smiled at his flush of embarrassment from his assumption. He'd hoped to deal man to man obviously. Maybe he'd hoped to get a better price from a man. He'd hoped to leave with a great horse at a great price. Not going to happen now, and his look showed his disappointment. He couldn't possibly get a good deal from a woman.

"Uhm, yeah, I'm sorry if I came at a bad time. I'm here about…" He nervously glanced down at the post it he fiddled with, a hint of pink touching his cheeks.

"Winks?"

His brows rose and fell with the name. I laughed. "Nickname. He winks." I shrugged and motioned him to the barn. Reba left us to business and returned to the foal pasture, wandering the fence line and marking it on her daily rounds.

"You have some nice looking foals out there." The stranger's long stride kept up easily with my quick steps. I could feel his curious gaze on my back.

"Thanks. Let me call Winks up. I'll get him saddled for you. You can take him around the arena, see how he rides." I waited at the door, glancing over my shoulder when his footsteps silenced. As I turned, his eyes moved up from below my waist to my eyes. I frowned.

"Uhm… sorry." He turned his gaze to the few squares of hay on the feed floor, "You, uh, have hay for sale?" He lifted his black felt hat from his head and ran his free hand over his thick, wavy hair, pushing a few too long strands behind his ears before replacing his hat.

"You're not here for Winks?"

"Uhm... well... I'm needing hay." He stammered.

"Well, I don't have much right now. I'll have a little more near the end of the month."

"How much can you spare?" He cleared his throat, deepened his voice.

I turned. "Look mister, I'm a very busy woman. Did you call me about the horse just to see if I had hay? I have about 50 bales I could sell right now, and one very mischievous horse. And you don't have to be all embarrassed about checking me out. You're not the first guy in the world to do that. I'll be right back." I pulled Winks' halter and lead down, welcoming the leave of absence from this curious man's foolishness. As I left the barn—head shaking— I fought to hold back my emotions. I couldn't decide whether to laugh or cry. Did this guy even know what he wanted?

Returning with Winks in tow, I laid his lead over a stall rail, lightly brushed the grass and dust off him where he'd rolled when I turned him out hours earlier, and threw the blanket over his back. The saddle fell easily in place, and I bent to pick up each hoof to make sure he hadn't collected any stones in the pasture. Stones could maim a horse if left stuck under a shoe.

My back to the stranger, I caught his searching gaze again as I raised up from inspecting the last hoof. I was beginning to think he'd never seen a woman before, at least not the backside of a woman. I can't say that a tingle of delight didn't filter through me at the thought of him trying to imagine me without clothes. It had been a while since I'd felt that particular attraction.

"Okay, look. Let's try to keep this business-like, shall we?" I bridled Winks and handed him the reins.

"Uh, no, you ride him. I, uhm, am better watching," he stammered.

Tilting my head, I looked up into his eyes, deep blue with flecks of green and hints of golden brown. He looked away quickly. "Who? Him or *me*?" My brows drew together in frustration. I didn't know what game he was playing, but I had a good mind to grab his face and give him a nice, long kiss. He'd probably leave, without horse or hay. I smiled just as his eyes landed on mine, again.

"Okay, mister, you win." I led Winks out of the barn into the arena. The stranger followed, leaning his tall frame against the panel, propping one boot heel on the bottom rail. He pushed his hat toward the back of his head so it wouldn't interfere with his view and nodded a thin, shy smile at me when I looked his way.

Seriously? Was he really that shy, or was he uncomfortable? He almost acted like he wasn't who I thought he was. Was he?

While I rode Winks around the arena, galloping, jumping, backing and putting on a sale show, my thoughts turned to this stranger's arrival. He'd said he wanted to buy a horse for his daughter, hadn't he? I'd read so many emails since the day I listed Winks. I road over as close to the panel as I could. His hands thumbed his front pockets, his elbows resting on the fence rail. No ring; no tan line.

"What do you think?" I halted before him, and his eyes quickly blinked from me to Winks.

Shielding his eyes from the sun behind me, he returned his attention to my face. "I think you ride very well." He nodded, stroking Winks' long nose. I didn't know if he was talking to me or the horse.

"Look… are you sure you don't want to take him around the arena a couple of times? I've been riding most of my life, except for a few years, when I lived in the city. A good rider can fool a buyer. A serious buyer rides for himself."

"Yeah… I'm not much of a rider… cattle." He stretched a hand forward and caressed Winks' long nose hypnotically. What interest did he have in a horse then? He didn't act as if he even really want to buy a horse. "Would you mind taking him around one more time?"

A curious request from a curious man, I thought. "Sure. Whatever you want. Watch closely now." I added sarcastically as I shook my head, annoyed at the request. This strange man, this rude man who never gave his name, was really starting to annoy me. I decided to keep my eyes away from the panel, away from him and just ride. I'd been on Winks for a while before Reba's bark pulled me out of the trance I sometimes entered while riding. I could get on a horse and lose track of time so easily.

One day, after I quit my job in the city, I got on my favorite mare and rode all day, just to keep my mind off of the accident. We rode, rested, rode all day.

I stopped Winks. He was starting to get warm; his neck damp beneath my rubbing hand. "Just a little longer, Winks. Maybe if we stay out here, that odd man will leave." Winks' ears flicked backward, then forward again, as if agreeing with me.

"So, that Winks you're on?" A different voice, much deeper, much more confident of himself called out. What? A girl's voice, probably Rachel's age, followed the man's, "Oh, Daddy, he's beautiful! I want him, Daddy, please?" Not at all spoiled. Great! This was going to be a deal breaker. I wouldn't sell to just anyone.

But if this was the man who emailed about Winks, then who was that strange—albeit incredibly attractive —guy? I turned Winks to the panel—barn side— and walked him over.

The first man was gone. I looked down the driveway, seeing nothing. Okay, I told myself, strange guy, strange day, let's just get this no-deal over with.

"I take it you jump? You said that's why you wanted him."

"She does." The man nodded as he approached the horse, brows drawn in contemplation as he held out his ringed left hand to help me down.

"Good, let's see what you can do. He's a little damp, so go easy. Another interested party just left." I told the girl.

"We didn't pass anyone coming in." The smug man replied, as if I was attempting to create a bid war. I frowned at him in warning.

"Yes, ma'am!" The young girl placed foot in stirrup, easily pulling herself up and over. Her dad adjusted the stirrups, though not much, and moved away to lean on the panels.

"She loves to ride," he remarked; his words reinforced by the way she moved. Another natural, I was more worried now about how she would treat Winks. She returned within minutes, Winks huffing slightly as she stopped him before us and patted his neck, "Good boy. You're perfect Winks, just perfect!" Then she leaned forward and hugged him, her head resting easily at the middle of his long neck. "You're so warm. Let's cool you down, boy!" She jumped from the saddle, pulled the reins over his head and led him to the panel, "Where's his halter?"

I smiled. He was getting a good home. "Just inside the barn door. I'll get it."

She scratched his nose, hugged him again, and placed her hand over his nose; his head rested over her shoulder as she stroked and scratched. He was doomed for spoiling, too; I could tell.

"Does he eat treats?" she called.

"And everything else he gets his mouth on… laundry, watermelon, dog food…" I think subconsciously I was trying to change her mind, but she only laughed.

"A character!" She placed her palm beneath his mouth, a round oat treat resting there for him. He gobbled it, and then proceeded to show her what a character he could be by nibbling on her ponytail.

"Oh, yeah, and hair," I called. She giggled, pushing him away playfully. She haltered him quickly and led him around the pen while her dad and I talked price. He was not as easy on women as the mystery man would have been. This guy was all business.

"Sir, I can't take less than my price. He's show ready. She won't have any problems with that one." I shook my head at him.

"Well, I hope you're right. The last one threw her and liked to killed her mother." He winced.

"Her mother rides also?"

"Oh, no! She almost died of a heart attack when her only child came off the horse and landed in the sand." He clarified.

"Oh, I see." I smiled at his recount. "Well, if you have any problems with him, bring him back. I'll refund your money."

"You'll guarantee that horse?" He watched his daughter walking the big animal around the arena, talking to him like he was her long, lost friend. Winks was in love; he wasn't coming home and I knew it. One treat and he gave it all up to some little kid. He was such a sucker. A guaranty wasn't going to be an issue.

"Yessir, I will, but I don't think you'll have any trouble out of him." I raised my left foot behind me and hooked the heel on the bottom rail. I crossed my arms over my chest watching this tall man's daughter spoil Winks while her father reasoned out a way he might get the price lowered.

"Eh… I think you're right." He said after a few minutes. "Okay, it's a deal." He pulled his checkbook free from his back pocket and flipped it open to write out the check. "By the way, you have a bit of a grease smudge on your left cheek," the man nodded toward the smudge before handing the payment to me.

"I do? Well!" I rubbed at it with my left hand.

We shook hands and I watched as the girl led Winks to their trailer. Winks turned one last time, snorted his good bye, and pushed at the little girl's back with his nose after she opened the trailer door as if he was telling her, "Hurry up, get me in there before that crazy woman starts crying!"

And I did, cry… balloon payment check in hand and tears rolling down my cheeks. At times all the trouble of raising horses, training them and selling them was more painful than it was worth. As I headed into the house with the check, I wondered if I did this to torture myself more over the accident all that time ago. I put the check in the fireproof box in anticipation of my weekly Monday trip into town and returned to the tractor, Mystery Man returning to my thoughts.

Who the hell was that guy? Was he really here just to buy hay and maybe got too embarrassed about his incorrect assumption? Whatever brought him to my ranch, there was a familiar look to him. He reminded me of someone, but I couldn't think who it was. Nevertheless, he was very attractive… dangerously attractive. I needed to watch my step with guys like that.

Tractor running, disks hooked up, I headed for the back pasture where I spent the rest of the afternoon and evening preparing it for seeding.

Darkness fell too soon, but Rachel had the horses fed before the tractor bounced me back to the equipment barn. Rachel ran out to help me, opening and closing the gates, her sad face peering up at my tired one. I parked the tractor and climbed down.

My stomach rumbled. Another day that I kept myself so busy I had forgotten to eat. "Don't be sad. It's what I do, Rach," I squeezed her shoulders in a one arm hug. I'd watched Rachel feed a few times, and each day she walked the length of the feed troughs and stroked each horse's nose. She loved each of them as much as I did.

"I know, but I miss him." She rested her head on my shoulder, a warm tear leaving a dark spot of my shirt. I let her go.

"Trooper's still here, waiting for the day you take him home!" I tilted my head so I could see her face, then

I pulled the pink cap off my head and let my long, damp hair out of its restraint. The creeping dusk brought a chill to the air and I shivered as it sought my damp head.

"I know, and I can't wait for that day!" She perked up, "How much longer will it be?"

"Hmm," I pretended to calculate, one index finger writing numbers and signs in the air, "eight years, four months and three days." I nodded, "Yeah, that should do it."

"What? Eight years!" She threw her head back with a whack of her palm on her forehead. "I'll be graduated by then! I won't have time to ride! I'll be in college! Eight years?"

I laughed at her dramatics. Why had I said that? The numbers fell from my tongue so easily. "Silly girl! You're almost there. I'd say, actually, maybe a year."

"Really? Oh, boy!"

"You better get home before the coyotes start moving through that brush. Take Reba with you," I pushed Rachel toward the fence, a few stars already twinkling above us. "Reba!"

The ghostly dog squeezed herself under the gate and headed for Rachel's worn footpath, stopping to wait for the pre teen on the other side of the fence. "See ya tomorrow, Andi," Rachel waved.

My stomach rumbled again. Fresh air and hard work always made me incredibly hungry.

"You know, Mom would love for you to come to dinner!" Rachel answered my stomach's loud request over her shoulder.

"Thank her for me. Bye, Rach!" I watched until I could no longer see Reba's bright frame in the rising moonlight. Pausing in the carport to wait for Reba's return home, I rolled my tired neck a few times, the vertebrae popping easily. After Reba returned for her treat, I scratched her behind the ears, which brought to mind the Mystery Man standing by the tractor earlier.

Who was that guy? Why did he disappear like that?

The kitchen was dark when I entered the back door. I'd forgotten to leave any lights on. Only the light from the carport stretched into the kitchen from open door frame. I flipped the switch next to the back door, illuminating the dark kitchen and parts of the living room. As hot water gushed from the open faucet, I squirted some soap into my hands and scrubbed them until they were pink from the temperature. I thought about taking a shower. I needed one badly, but my stomach responded loudly in opposition. Food, then shower, I assured my stomach as I dried my hands on a dish towel where two turkeys met a fall colored background in anticipation of Thanksgiving. Thanksgiving was a month away. That's how little attention I paid to decor in my home. I didn't have time for interior decorating.

Pulling the freezer drawer open, I noted my selection of frozen dinners had diminished quicker than expected. I specifically purchased them for long days like today. I loved to cook, but had little reason or time to do so. I pulled a meal from the freezer, flipped it upright, and turned on the oven to preheat it. When was the last time I had cooked my dinner? What did I have then? I frowned in thought as I returned for a beverage—wine or beer? Beer, and maybe I'd have more than one tonight. I twisted the top from the bottle and tossed the top in the trash can before taking a long swallow of the icy cold, golden liquid. An almost instant rush of lightheadedness filled me, a giddiness that washed away the events of the day and the nightmare I awoke to. That was exactly what I wanted. Tonight, I would drive away the memories of Winks, and the accident, with a beer or two.

The oven beeped its readiness and I opened it, placed the frozen dinner on the top rack and closed the door. I set the shut off timer, knowing if I didn't, I would forget and burn another dinner. The beer tasted so good that I finished it before I left the kitchen, threw away the bottle, and pulled another from the fridge. This one would last longer, though I had two much to drown tonight: that spoked tire and this morning's show being the last comfort Winks would offer my mornings.

I forced the crazy voice from my head along with the accident and took another swallow of beer. Then I pushed all thoughts from my head. I sat in my recliner, remote in hand, and clicked the on button. The station I'd left on the night before jarred my eyes open. Had I left it that loud? By the light of the kitchen, I focused my already blurring eyes on the volume button and pushed the downward arrow. George Strait's voice sang me away to another place, his songs just low enough that I could still hear the oven timer, but not so low that the beer had to do its job alone. The King of Country brought stories to my mind and kept me from thinking of anything else that had happened during that day. I closed my eyes, leaned my head back into the overstuffed softness of my favorite leather chair, and sang along to my favorite song, tilting the bottle to my lips between bars, imagining myself in *Marina Del Rey*.

I dozed off, half a beer still in hand, feet up, until the timer on the oven woke me. Lowering the chair to its normal position, I rose, gripped the bottle, and started for the kitchen. I didn't even make it all the way in before the beer slipped from my hand to the floor at my feet, its contents spreading quickly along the plane of vinyl flooring toward the center of the house.

My jaw hung open.

The oven beeped again.

Speechless, I stared; my stocking feet frozen to the floor.

Mystery Man stood inside my house at the other end of the kitchen, just inside the door to the carport.

I tried to scream, but my throat would not release the desperate noise I felt within.

"I'm sorry." He spoke softly, raising his hands in a "don't shoot me" action before moving quickly to clean up the spreading wet spot. "I'll get that for you!" He grabbed the turkey towel from the counter and spread it over the beer, catching the running liquid just before it crept under the refrigerator. "I knocked. I called to you. I could hear the music, so I didn't think you heard me." He nervously wiped at the beer while I stared at the back of his head beneath me wondering whether to knee him in the nose or jump on his back.

I searched for my cell phone, which was nowhere in sight. Stay calm, I told myself, breathing slowly, deeply in, then out. "So, you just walked into my house? A stranger? I could have shot you!" I panicked.

"Not likely. You were snoring a little." He tilted his head back to look up at me and grimaced.

"Snoring? I was snor... what are you doing in my house?" I side-stepped the beer flowing freely toward me as he pushed at it with the towel. Slowly I moved around the island toward the back door. No weapon at hand, cell phone on the charger, the next best thing was Reba. Moving quickly while he was distracted, I opened the back door where she lay on the porch, and motioned her inside. She rolled onto her back and looked at me upside down. Then she eyed Mystery Man bent over and jumped up.

How had he gotten past her?

Reba scrambled into the house, head down, sniffing the floor, ready to pounce on the intruder; and just as he turned to ask for another towel, she licked his face, then turned her tongue to the escaping beer.

"Fat lotta protector you are!" I told the white fluff.

Reba raised a large paw and placed in on the man's shoulder. She stood on her hind legs, pushing the man to the floor, then licked furiously at his perfect chin and his strong cheek bones. A child-like giggle sounded from his throat. "Stop. Stop." He fought to turn away from her, his butt planted firmly in the portion of beer yet to be cleaned up.

"Reba!" I called, yet while she distracted him, I reached for the broom.

"Call her off, will ya?" He laughed, deeper this time, more manly. His laugh touched something inside me, somewhere at the pit of my stomach. "Oh, come on! First your dog licks me to death and then you beat me with a broom? Give me a break!" He took both Reba's front paws from his chest and placed them on the floor, soon after pushing Reba's ready tongue away as he rolled to the side and stood up.

"What do you expect? A hug? You're in my house! You're a stranger—who never told me his name by the way—and you're in my house!" I raised the broom over my head.

"I'm sorry. I know. Put the broom down, please. Andi, please?"

"Don't call me, Andi. You don't know me. I don't know you. We are not friends."

"But, you told me," his brows rose. "Earlier, out there."

"My God! Who the hell are you?" I finally lost it. His nerve, barging into my home, not telling me who he was, infuriated me, and him making nice with my dog? Seriously?

The oven timer beeped in the background adding to my frustration.

"You gonna get that?" He nodded to the oven.

The breath I'd been holding released in a rush as the broom crashed to the floor. I pushed the timer button with one finger, the off button with another— even though it turned off automatically— and lunged toward him, so angry I no longer needed the broom. I was ready to kill him with my bare hands!

He reeked of warm beer as I flew at him in a rage. Fisted hands fell on him as I screamed like a banshee. Reba jumped at the same time as my hands fell close to his shoulders, knocking me to the floor. I glared at her, but she panted at me, her brown eyes pointing me toward my chair and back to me as if to say, "You're dreaming. Wake up." Her calmness transferred to me, and I ruffled the soft fur around her head, kissed her nose and rose, my jeans also now soaked from the beer on the floor. I expected when I turned that he would be gone, like earlier at the barn, a figment of my imagination, a dream after a hard day, but he was still there.

Was I dreaming?

I gave up, shrugged, and returned to my chair, plopping down with a huff, rubbing my eyes, and resting my elbows on my knees.

I looked again.

He was still standing there. "Do you have another towel? Or maybe a mop?"

My lips made an O and I blew out a breath. "In the pantry."

He was still here. Why was he here? I shook my head. Reba appeared before me, licked my nose, and sat. "You're okay," her soft brown eyes assured me. She had become my untrained therapy dog.

"You sure about that?" I asked Reba aloud.

"Sure about what?" he asked me.

"Nothing. I wasn't talking to you. As a matter of fact, anything I say from this point on, is not directed at you. You are not here," I peered out the dark window beside me.

"You sure about that?" He repeated my question.

My mouth opened in reply, but I snapped it shut. He was really getting on my nerves. Don't look at him. Don't acknowledge him. He's all in your mind. He's not real.

Then what about my dog? She sees him, too.

She's not real, either, I told myself. You're dreaming. Heck, for all you know you're having another meltdown!

Reba licked my nose, again. I wiped the wet spot she left behind. It was real.

But was he?

Finished with the task of cleaning up beer, I watched from the corner of my eye as his long legs moved toward the living room. His boots scraped quietly on the laminate flooring.

I shut my eyes, squeezing them tightly closed. Involuntarily my head shook from side to side.

"You're not crazy, Andi…" His hand appeared, palm up, beneath my nose, "…but you are extremely beautiful." Reba stepped lightly away from me, her feet padding to the front door, as George Strait sang *I Saw God Today* in the background.

I blinked, but his hand was still there.

"Dance with me, Andi."

"I don't even know you."

Numbness filled my body. I'd lost it. I gave in; in part because I was sure it was a fantasy dream… and there was the fact that he was extremely charming, attractive, and chiseled. I laid my hand in his and rose from my chair. He pulled me close, his shoulder resting my cheek, his waist tightly pushed into my upper abdomen. His body moved gracefully as he floated me around the living room.

The numbness dissipated, replaced by a tingle spreading from my left hand where it rested between his shoulders, down my forearm, to my elbow, and up to my shoulder. It traveled through me, head to toe, a warm, lost sensation that would be gone too soon when I returned to reality.

The song played out, the dream almost over, his chin resting lightly on my head. I spoke softly into his chest, "Who are you? Do you have a name?"

His soft laugh tickled my ear drum, replacing the solid beat of his heart, "Of course I do."

"Well?" I lifted my head from his chest as the song ended and looked up into his smiling eyes. He seemed to have changed since the afternoon, no longer embarrassed by staring at me. There was a boldness there that I hadn't seen earlier. His eyes roamed freely about my face, a corner of his lip raised, and his gaze landed wantonly on my lips, which magnetically drew closer in response. One light kiss, soft, warm, filled with desire.

This is a dream, I decided.

"Did you sell him… Winks?"

I peered into his playful eyes, "Yes. Why won't you tell me who you are?"

"Does it really matter, my name?"

"Until I know your name, you're a stranger. I don't kiss strangers."

"You just did." He leaned forward and kissed me again. "Again."

"Are you hiding something from me?" I asked as we moved to a song I don't remember hearing.

"I have nothing to hide."

"Then tell me your name," I pleaded.

His phone vibrated in his pocket, pulsing into my hip and downward. "Are you gonna get that?"

A knowing smile turned his lips, "Should I?" He raised his brows. I pushed away.

"Yes, you should, Mr... ?"

"All right... all right, Cole." He laughed playfully as his grip tightened on my hand and he pulled me back into him.

"Have we met before, Mr. Cole?" I had frequented a few bars in the past, with friends, when I didn't have to drive. I scoured my brain, trying to remember his name.

"Mmm... not really." He peered down into my face, wrapping his arm across my shoulders, anticipating the next song. His phone vibrated again.

"Okay, look. Somebody is obviously trying to reach you." I pushed away again, pulling my hand free of his.

"I know."

I moved backward a few steps, and he followed.

"A wife. It's a wife. Why did you come here this afternoon?" The unchanging look on his face scared me a little, though I didn't feel threatened. After all, it was all a dream. Nobody would actually enter the house of a stranger unless... he wasn't going to kill me! Reba loved him.

Maybe he was going to kill me and run off with my dog!

I kept backing away from him and he kept moving toward me. "Why did you come here?"

He smiled. How had he gained control of me so quickly? I picked up the broom, backed around the island, kept moving away from him. Backing myself into a door, he moved toward me, cupped my face between his two slightly calloused hands, and lowered his lips to mine, his tongue probed, searching for a way in. I wouldn't give in. I wouldn't let him have complete control, though my attraction to him was so strong I almost didn't care. I had to take back the control of actions even in my dreams. I didn't even know this guy. The vibration in his pocket startled me again as my mouth seceded to his seeking tongue.

What is wrong with you? My brain screamed at me. He's a stranger!

His hands released my face, he pulled away and smiled. Phone in hand, he checked the message and stated flatly, "It was nice to meet you, Andi. I'll be back tomorrow for those fifty bales." And I watched him let my dog out, following her into the darkness.

"Oh, and do me a favor. Close and lock that door after you let Reba in for the night!" He said over his shoulder.

The broom in my hand clattered noisily to the floor once again.

Hot water ran over my head and through the long wet hair flowing down my back.

I had eaten my cold dinner, locked my house up tight, and headed for the shower, where I now stood allowing the warmth to remove the grime of the day as well as the mental issues I'd dealt with.

It was my imagination, wasn't it? A lonely woman's dream?

You'll find out tomorrow if he comes to get the hay, right? I asked myself.

As tired as I was, the feeling of lying back on my sateen sheets and covering my nakedness with the bedcovers comforted me, but the dream intruder called for a different action. The last thing I needed was for him to come back tonight, break into my home, and find me naked between my sheets. For all I knew, Reba gave him a key to the house without a word to me. Oh, that dog!

I pulled on my flannel pajamas and fell back on my pillow, the strange day behind me, ready to start over tomorrow.

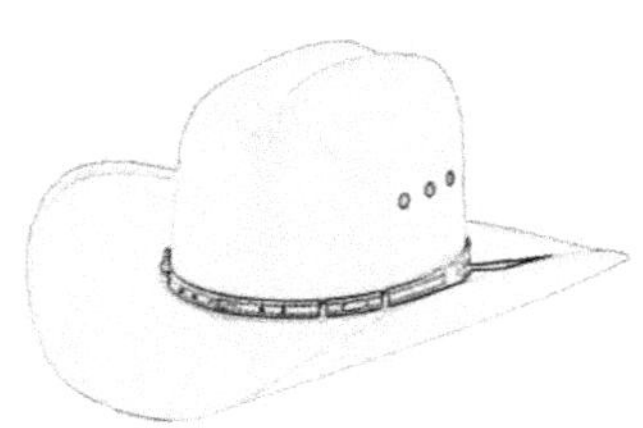

The tire rolled into my peripheral vision.
"BTW… I love you."
The screech of tires.
The neighbors pointing at me accusingly, angrily, the text

message flashing up at me.

I tossed and turned, my flesh damp with sweat.

I rolled over to get away from the nightmare.

Why? Why was it haunting me now?

No matter what I tried, I found no relief from the neighbors' accusing eyes until I awakened to the buzz of my phone on the nightstand.

Scooping it up, I slid my finger across the screen to unlock it and saw the #1 in the text message bubble. I looked at the time, 3:48 am. Ugh, who would text me at this hour?

I slammed the phone down on the nightstand.

3:48?

Why do those numbers seem familiar? I thought as my eyelids fell closed.

"Eight years, four months, three days!" That's what I told Rachel! My eyes popped open as I sat upright.

"Oh, come on!" I sighed falling back against the pillows, but it was too late, I was wide awake and left with a strange feeling.

Sitting up, I swung my legs over the side of the bed and reached for my phone now laying silent on the table. Unlocking it again, I touched the message icon. An odd set of numbers appeared where the name should have been, 84-384 and I imagined those three numbers going on and on for infinity. I touched the bubble to read the message.

"BTW… I love you."

The phone flew from my hand as I jumped out of bed; it bounced off the wall opposite me and crashed to the floor, sliding to a stop beneath the edge of my bed.

The voices in my head returned.

I couldn't lose it, again, but I felt the darkness returning. Who would do this? Who would send Matt's message to me?

Cole's face filled my mind.

Who was he?

Had he sent the message?

How would he have gotten my phone number? I didn't give it to him.

Did he know about the accident? Why would a stranger torture me like that unless he knew?

Questions without answers tore through my brain severing it down the middle.

Cole's touch as we danced had brought tingles to my body, but now as I remembered his caresses I shuddered with fear.

It couldn't be him! I tried clearing my head, remembering if I had locked the doors, the windows, too.

Breathe deeply.

Clear your mind.

Find the peacefulness behind your eyelids.

Breathe.

Within minutes, I returned to bed and to a welcoming sleep, the paranoia subsiding and dreams filling the darkness.

* * *

"All aboard, Andi!" Matt held the new bicycle upright with one hand while straddling a second new bicycle.

"Where did these come from?" I moved to hold up the riderless bike while stroking the new seat.

"I bought them yesterday. For us." He grinned widely delighted by the look on my face. I felt like a little girl who just woke up Christmas morning to find a new bike under the tree. Then my wonder filled expression faded.

"I have a confession to make. I never learned to ride a bike."

"What?! Are you kidding me? How could you grow up… better yet where did you grow up… that you didn't learn to ride a bike?"

"Well, not every child is raised the same way, Matt. I mean, I rode horses. And I think I had a tricycle. My parents were just busy… all the time."

"Wow!" Matt shook his head in disbelief. "Then I guess today is your lucky day." He turned to me with that playful look in his eyes. "I happen to be the best teacher of bicycle riding, so you just hop aboard right now." He turned his bicycle and found a level place to park it, then walked over to mine.

"I don't think so Matt. Right here? In the parking lot? What if I fall over… and a car pulls in… and…"

"You won't. Now get on!"

I straddled the bike and sat back on the seat, "Are you sure you can teach me how to ride?"

Holding the back of the seat to stabilize the bike, he leaned over my shoulder and whispered, "No, but I'll try. You can be somewhat of a challenge, you know." Then he moved my hair and kissed my neck.

"Stop!" I leaned away from him. "I'm serious! What if I break an arm or leg or something!"

"Hmm… or something is most likely, but you won't know until you try. Now, feet on the pedals!" Matt ordered.

The bicycle wobbled beneath me and I put my feet down to balance it.

"Once you start peddling, it will be easier to balance," Matt informed me.

"Are you sure?" I did not want to fall over.

"Yes! And I will be holding on until you balance. Feet on the pedals!" I followed his instruction. "Now, pedal, just like you're using a stationary bike! Go!"

I pushed down reluctantly on the right pedal, then the left, then the right. I could feel Matt's hand on the back of the seat helping to keep the wandering bike steady. Then, his hand was gone and I was riding the bike around the near empty dorm parking lot. Before I could contain my excitement, Matt was riding next to me.

"See, best bicycle riding teacher in the world!" Matt boasted.

"Oh, yes, you are the best!" I agreed facetiously. Then, I let go of the handle bars and leaned back allowing my balance to steer the bike.

"Hey! That's… Wait! You knew how to ride all along, didn't you?" Matt pursed his lips.

Hands returned to the bars, I smiled, "Just a little." I turned away and raced down the bike path.

A pounding noise filled my ears. I squinted against the bright sunlight cutting through my slitted blinds.

Rolling away from the light, I pulled the covers over my head. I didn't want to wake up, yet... maybe ever.

"Andi! Andi, are you okay?"

Rachel?

I threw the comforter back as my eyes opened in concern. *Oh, no! I overslept.*

I rushed to the front door, unlocking it, and flinging it open.

"Rachel! I'm so sorry. I overslept. Come in. I'll get dressed."

"No hurry. I fed for you. Are you okay? Are you sick? Want me to make your coffee?"

I froze in my bedroom door and turned, "You can do that? You're twelve years old."

"Sure, I make coffee for my dad sometimes. Take your time. I'll get it for you." Rachel rummaged through the cabinet above the coffee maker. "You seem really weird today. Are you sick?" She asked again, looking at me curiously. She filled the pot and poured the water into the reservoir. I didn't have the heart to tell her I didn't drink a whole pot of coffee in the morning.

"No. No, I'm fine… I think." I closed the bedroom door behind me as she asked, "Can I get some juice?"

"Sure, help yourself!" I opened the door briefly with my answer, then went to get ready for the morning. I grabbed jeans and a shirt from my closet and slipped out of my jammies. The pile of clothes in the hamper reminded me I would have to do laundry later today. My hair brush lay next to the sink, and I plucked it up to run it through my hair. The brief glance in the mirror reflected the rough-night I'd had, bags, dark circles. No wonder she thought I was sick. Splashing the icy water over my face caused me to suck in a sharp breath, but I did it a second time anyway, then plucked a towel from the rack to pat my face dry.

Calm down. Deep breaths— in, out.

It was all a dream, a very weird, scary dream.

Deep breath— in, out.

My hands reached shakily for the brush on my counter and pulled it through my hair a second time. More deep breaths and I was calm enough to leave the room where the aroma of hot coffee drew my attention as I exited the bedroom door.

"Boy, did you tie one on last night or something? You look rough!" Rachel took a sip of orange juice.

"Yeah, maybe I did," I opened the fridge for

creamer and discovered only the two beers missing that I removed the night before, "or not."

"Huh?"

"Nothing," I poured my coffee, thinking about the text message on my phone, the strange number, and Mr. Cole, the Mystery Man of Hay. "Hey, Rach, did you happen to notice a vehicle here yesterday?" I stared out the window at the gravel road down the end of my driveway as I sipped coffee. Mac would be disappointed this morning missing her morning coffee. Of course, there would be no show to watch, either.

"You mean the people who bought Winks? That's the only truck I saw. Are you sure you're okay, Andi?"

"Yeah, hon. Yeah, I'm fine." I wanted to talk about it, but how was I going to talk to a twelve year old girl about a guy who came into my home uninvited and who may not even exist?

Rachel didn't know about my accident with the bicycle, so I couldn't tell her about the text message. Heck, she wasn't even old enough to remember the accident if she had heard about it… I don't think. When was it?

I would never tell Rachel about it, anyway. I didn't even want to think about it!

"We don't have to ride today, if you don't feel like it." Rachel moved to the sink and looked up at me, her glass of juice poised at her lips.

"Of course, we do! You need to be ready by spring. Just… just let me finish my coffee. Drink your juice." I turned away from her, set my coffee on the island, and slipped into my socks and boots.

"You're acting really strange, Andi. Want me to get

Mom?"

"No! No." I got control of myself and looked directly into her eyes. "I just had some odd dreams. I guess they left me feeling kind of, well, off." Returning to the coffee pot, I topped my cup, turned off the pot, and motioned Rachel toward the door.

"Okay, okay!" She chugged the last bit of her juice and followed. I drank three quarters of my coffee cup and left the rest on the table for Mac, even though she was no where to be seen. Reba ran up to me, tail wagging, bouncing like she hadn't seen me all night. Looking down at her, I reached over and patted her head, whispering, "Traitor," and she followed as we headed to the barn. I glanced at the foal pasture on the way to the barn. I had missed their morning show, but it wouldn't be the same without Winks, anyway.

"You're gonna miss him, too. Worse than me," Rachel's voice quivered.

"It's part of the job, Rachel. I am going to miss him, but he has a good home and nothing bad will happen to him. I have to believe that."

"How'dya know?" She plucked a tall piece of grass as she walked by, and waved it before her like a magic wand as she walked.

"Because, my little prodigy, they paid dearly for him. He will be taken care of." I put my arm across her shoulder and squeezed.

"I will never sell Trooper. I'll keep him forever!"

I looked down at her tanned face. "I hope you do."

"Who are you going to work with this morning?" She moved quickly through the barn, lifting Trooper's halter and lead, stopping at the door, awaiting my reply.

"Hmm...I don't know. Thunder, maybe."

She turned, her blue eyes wide, "Thunder?" her face fell.

"Yeah, I'm feeling a little daring this morning," I pursed my lips and nodded.

"What if he bucks you off?"

"He might just do that. I won't know until I try him… again." He had bucked me off the first time. He was a feisty three year old with too much energy and a mind of his own.

Reluctantly, she removed Thunder's halter and lead, slowly holding them out in my direction. I laughed. "You silly, silly girl! How do you think I got where I am in this business? I've been thrown off the back of more horses than I can count." I chuckled. Thunder was different, though. I was beginning to think he would be a better bronc horse than anything else. I wouldn't tell Rachel, but sometimes, Thunder even scared me.

I took the equipment from her with one hand and her curly blonde ponytail with the other. "Come on!" I directed her out the door after tugging a curl of her hair to watch it bounce back. With a nod of encouragement, I swung the pasture side door open and waited for Rachel to pass through before I headed in the opposite direction to halter Thunder. With the hand holding the halter behind my back, I eased up on the large horse. His head jerked back as I reached out to stroke his nose, "Easy. Easy, boy!" I cooed, gently reaching out and touching his nose. "Good morning, big fella!" I whispered.

Thunder calmed down. He had always spooked easily. Since the first time I'd put a halter on him when he was six months old, I had to sneak up to him. After a few minutes of cooing and stroking, Thunder allowed me to halter him. I don't know what made him so skittish as a foal, but he never outgrew it.

At the barn, Rachel unbuckled Trooper's halter and replaced it with his bridle. She'd already had him dressed out before I led Thunder into the barn. I tied Thunder near the door to the arena so he could watch as Rachel warmed Trooper up before running the pattern. She'd taken every instruction I gave her to heart and had learned well how to ride that pattern.

"You see that, boy? I know you can do that, Thunder. We just need to calm you down." I talked to the fifteen and a half hand gelding, brushing and stroking him as Trooper galloped near. Thunder snorted in response to Trooper's proximity, his front hooves stomping and pawing the dirt below him. Trooper never flinched in reply. Again, I wondered what could have happened to Thunder to cause his high anxieties. He acted so much like a stud that all I could assume was he'd been gelded too late. Each horse was different, though, just like each person was different.

The main goal I wanted to accomplish with Thunder was picking up his feet before he was dressed out. He was still a booger about his feet and liked to cow-kick the farrier every time I called the poor man out to shoe the horses.

Brush out completed and dust removed, I cautiously placed his pad and saddle on his back. The motion of placing the items loosely on his back made him quiver and nicker. By the time I had him dressed out, Rachel had run the pattern a few times and was cooling down Trooper. I buckled and tightened a little at a time as Thunder danced, his muscular body tensing when Rachel's mother called over the fence. The big bay flinched, turned toward the sound, perked his head, and nickered frantically.

"Easy, boy. Easy does it..." I stroked his neck, patted and calmed him.

Thunder was a beautiful horse, but if I didn't get him calmed down, he wouldn't sell at all... well, except to a rodeo crew. Some people liked a horse with a little fire, but few wanted to die while riding a horse.

Thunder's chestnut body relaxed under my touch as I talked to him and stroked his neck, "It's Rachel's mom. It's okay." I watched his right eye closely until he focused it on me and turned forward as if to say to me, "Oh, it's you bugging me, again."

"Hello?" The neighbor called in the barn entrance.

"Come on in. Rachel's just cooling Trooper down." I replied softly, evenly; as I stroked the anxious gelding on his neck, his socked feet stomped and fidgeted. "Slowly," I told Rachel's mother.

"Andi, I don't know how you do it. That horse looks crazy!" She answered with a quiet urgency while staring at the white showing in Thunder's eye.

"Hey, Mom," Rachel whispered from the arena side. She knew the routine with Thunder and went around the barn instead of bringing Trooper through it. Once, Thunder had almost kicked her while trying to strike Trooper. "Come on, Mom," Rachel motioned.

"Hmm, I guess it's a no on lunch again, Andi? Looks like you have your hands full today." The slender woman added.

"Maybe next time," I assured her.

"I'll be back to check on you in an hour, Andi," Rachel stated.

"Uh, no you won't, Rach. We have to go to Gramma's this afternoon," her mother reminded.

"But, Mom, Thunder could kill Andi and we wouldn't know!" Rachel argued.

I chuckled as I calmed the huge bay.

"Stop being so melodramatic!" Her mother scolded. "You're not getting out of going to your gramma's. Bye, Andi!" The soft spoken woman called quietly over her shoulder.

"Bye. Have a nice visit," I whispered over Thunder's back, all the while stroking him as if it were him I was speaking to.

The quiet arguing of mother and daughter grew further away as I ran my hand down the leg of the now calm beast at my fingertips. I rose, looked in his eye where no white showed. His feet solid on the ground, his rapid breathing slowed. He was such a beautiful horse; a complete opposite of the personality of Winks and a little slower to learn, but he was still beautiful. His conformation alone would bring more if I could just get him to trust people. I just couldn't understand the mistrust. He was raised here. I've never even looked at him wrong. I wondered if horses could have mental illness like people did... like I did. Maybe that's why I never gave up on him.

I slid my hand down his left front leg, placing it on the front of his hoof and to my surprise, he picked up his foot and rested it in my hand. "One down, three to go," I quietly praised him as I picked out dried mud and twigs.

I worked my way around, about to pick up his right front, when his shoulder flinched and his head tightened the tied lead rope as he looked over my back. My hand halfway down his leg, I froze, waiting for him to go nuts, but he didn't. He strained to look at something behind me.

"Mhm, that is a beautiful sight!" A familiar voice quietly commented. The hair on my neck prickled.

"Don't move, please," I said flatly, as if calming Thunder. I had to finish the task at hand. Thunder returned his head to the forward position and my hand lightly travelled down his leg to the front of his hoof. My head remained well out of the way just in case. The large hoof lifted and fell gently into my palm. I cleaned it and let it down; a sigh of relief escaped my lips as I straightened my body and patted him softly on the neck, "You are getting so much better at this. You're such a good boy," I spoke softly, stroking his neck, watching his ears flick and listen with each gently touch. He blinked twice, completely calm.

"That is one massive animal," Cole whispered in awe.

"So... you are real," was my flat reply as I undressed Thunder.

"Of course I am. What do you mean by that?" The puzzled words made me look up at him while I placed the saddle on the rack. He showed no hint of anything happening between us the night before. I turned away from him, tugging the loop free on the lead rope before Thunder followed me out the side door.

When I returned, Cole stood in the doorway

smiling. "You really have a way with horses."

I searched his face, "Yeah, I suppose I do. If you'll bring your truck and trailer out here, I'll guide you out to the hay barn. The hay for sale is back there."

"Huh?" I brushed past him in the doorway to take the lead so I could open the gates for him to drive through, but his hand grasped my shirt tail, and he spun me around into his arms. "Look, Andi, about last night —" he started.

"Then you were here last night?"

"That depends. If I say no, does that mean you dreamt about me?" His brows rose playfully. I was not amused. "Okay, yeah, I came back last night to talk to you about the hay, and I guess I shouldn't have. I mean, you don't know me from the man at the grocery store," he shrugged.

"Yet, I know the man at the grocery store but you stand here with your arms around me holding me like we've been together forever and Ben would never..." My face remained cold and distant as I stared into his eyes and pushed at his firm arms.

"Ben?" He frowned in question.

"The man at the grocery store."

"Oh. Look, I couldn't help myself... you're just... you have the most beautiful eyes I've had the pleasure to stare into. They drew me in instantly, like you were reaching down into my soul for something you were missing."

Smooth talker, I thought.

With one finger he lifted a strand of hair from my eyelash and moved it aside. "I just couldn't stop thinking about you yesterday and... well, I had to leave suddenly when I was here earlier so I didn't get to talk to you about the hay…

"And, truth be told, I used the hay for an excuse to see you again." His eyes moved left and right ever so slightly as his words trailed off.

"Are you telling me you don't need hay?" I felt my blood boiling working into an angry outburst.

"If I said I need you…" he started.

"Cut the crap," I interrupted his facetious retort and pushed his arms away from my waist. I wasn't going to play this love game with him, again. I hadn't been drinking this time and now I didn't even know if I could trust him.

All I really needed to know from him was if he had sent me the text message early this morning?

"I don't know you!" I stepped away.

Where had he come from?

"Mom, it will be fine. I will be fine!" I assured her for the umpteenth time as I taped the box on my bed closed. Matt had graduated with his MBA and was off to a full time position while he continued to work on his Masters. He found a quaint little flat in biking distance from the campus and the bank that hired him, and I was moving in with the man I loved more than life itself. Everything was going to be great!

"Andi, you don't even know him. You've only been dating for a few months…" my mother pressed.

"Almost a year, Mom," I corrected.

"Still, you haven't finished school! What if you don't…"

"I will Mom. I'm going to get my Masters. Stop worrying. I'll be fine." I begged her to stop arguing.

"But you're not… you're not married, Andi." And there it was, her real reason for this protest.

"We're getting married Mom!" I waved the flashy diamond ring on my left hand before her eyes.

"But that's not the…"

"Mom! Please, stop. Just stop." I held the box between us as I raised my brows at her.

"Okay. Do what you want." She turned and left my bedroom.

After I carried the last box to my car, I returned to give her a hug. It was bad enough I had started college that year, but now I was moving out of the house. "I love you, Mom. I'll be home, again."

"I love you." Mom held me tightly. "And Andi, please don't get pregnant."

I pushed away from her. "Mom! That's the furthest thing from my plans! Really, one word Mom— contraceptives." I put my hand on her shoulder as if educating her to the ways of today's world.

"Andi, for Heaven's sake!"

"I'll be fine. I'll call you every weekend and we'll visit on the holidays. Please relax. There's no need to worry."

But there was… need for worry, not about me, about her.

Cole wouldn't answer any of my questions if I had asked them aloud. I started for the side exit of the barn beyond the stalls; his long stride closed in the distance I'd put between us. "Okay, look, I really do need hay for my cows. You're the only one I've heard of that has some to spare. But... I also have a question for you."

Before I reached the exit next to the tack room, he grasped my elbow and swung me around, again. His long fingers wrapped around my wrists as he leaned into me. His body felt so solid against mine that if the plywood wall behind me hadn't been there, I would have grabbed his waist to stay upright. His lips teased mine before gently forcing my mouth open to a fervent kiss that caused me to gasp, perhaps a slight moan escaped my throat. His kiss softened as my traitorous mouth gave into his. I felt my body giving way to his desire, yet I refused to give in. I stopped myself, resisting further kisses as his lips caressed my face. Releasing my wrists, he straightened, moved his hands to my face, caressed my hair with his fingers and my cheeks with his thumbs. "Have dinner with me tonight," he paused long enough to order me as if the thought had just occurred to him.

"That's not a question." I had a difficult time composing my voice; a slight quiver may have betrayed me. "Your truck. Your trailer. The hay." Nearly breathless, I reminded him cooly why he was at my ranch, though I desperately wanted him to kiss me again. A warmth spread over me that I hadn't felt since Matt. My spine tingled with desire. Still, I didn't know this man, and I didn't know if he was the one behind the text message that woke me briefly that morning.

He did kiss me again, longer, and this time I couldn't resist. I felt my knees tremble. I pressed my palms into the plywood behind me to stabilize my legs and keep them from wrapping around his neck. A light, gentle, tempting peck before he paused for breath, again, "Have dinner with me tonight." His face was so close our noses almost touched as he stared down into my eyes. I could feel his heated breath brushing my lips and I fought against the desire to kiss him back.

It was getting more difficult to maintain my business like composure. Inhaling deeply, I turned my face away and reestablished my emotionless stature—no hint of a smile or passion glimmered in my eyes—yet, my chest heaved and my shoulders and knees trembled beneath the facade.

"Have dinner with me tonight." He smiled this time, a crinkle at the corner of his eyes, a contagious, seductive, playful smile on his lips as though he knew I was struggling to hold back. "Have dinner with me tonight." He repeated, turning my face toward his again as his lips drew closer to my own.

Did I have a choice?

How could he be so forward and demanding with a woman he didn't know?

Was he the crazy one?

No matter what I told myself, the attraction was there—very real—and I knew he could feel the mutual yearning.

Remembering the text message, a plan formed in my mind and I acquiesced to his demand. I had to be near him more if I wanted to find out whether he was the text sender and why he would do it. Or, was my reasoning faulty and it was really desire that moved me to say yes?

Did he know about my accident, the text message, the person still lying in the hospital?

The game could get dangerous, so I needed to be careful, especially with this crazy attraction I felt. If he was the sender, there was no telling what he might do if I said no.

I would never know if I didn't agree with him.

Before I could answer, he repeated his request again.

"A public place," I calmly replied.

"Of course. Wherever you like." His lips touched mine again, lightly, then fervently one last time. "I would take you anywhere." And just like nothing had happened, again, he released me and walked through the open barn door. I was glad his back was to me as he walked away because my knees buckled and I nearly stumbled to the dirt floor. "Now, back to the hay... how much were you asking?" He turned as I regained my composure and stepped into the sunlight.

"Ten a bale," I answered without a stammer. Two could play at this game, though I hated to play it, but I hoped he hadn't heard the ragged breathe behind the words. "It's good quality coastal." I found it difficult it to get too close to him, so I maintained a distance beyond arms' length.

"Ten it is. Let's go load it!" He started toward his truck.

"Oh, I don't load the hay. You'll have to do that on your own!" Slightly annoyed with his shenanigans, I punctuated the comment with a shrug of my shoulders as I hurried past him to the gate.

"For ten a bale? What? Wait!" He quickly caught up with me and turned to face me. Walking backwards, he asked, "How'd you put it up?"

"I hire people. I just drive the tractor." A smug satisfaction filled me as his face twisted with thought. He hadn't seen Reba coming up behind him as he walked, but I had.

Hah!

"Hmm. Maybe I better bring some help, then. You know, five hundred is a lot for fifty bales I have to load myself. I can get it loaded at the feed store for eight."

"Then go to the feed store," I shrugged as if his comment made no difference to me.

"I did. They're out. Matter of fact, that's how I found out about you. Okay, you drive a tough bargain. I'll come back with help." Before he could turn his back to me, he backed over Reba who, which sheepish grin, enjoyed having put him on his backside. I turned away so he wouldn't see me laughing, and when he held his hand up to me for help, I moved past him.

"I can make a call, have the teenage boys down the road here to help you in five minutes," I offered.

"Well, that would be nice of you!" He stood, strode past me and turned back to tip his hat sarcastically.

"They only charge fifty cents a bale to load it… you know, teens and gas money…" I crinkled my nose again.

"What? That's another twenty-five dollars!" He feigned disbelief.

"You're pretty quick with math," I smiled and nodded.

"Whatever. Go ahead, call them." Defeated, he moved his truck forward and waited outside the drive-thru gate, motor running, phone to his ear. I wondered who he was talking to. Wife? Girlfriend? He was a fast moving one. He had to have some secret, other than the text message.

I also wondered what his phone number was. Of course, the numbers that showed this morning appeared to be from a service rather than an actual phone number.

Determined to go through with the dinner, to get close enough to him to do some snooping, I slipped into the house and found my cell phone under the bed—the text still showing from the wee hours—and virtually ran back outside.

Josh and his brother agreed to help, pulling into the driveway five minutes later as promised. I hopped onto the flatbed trailer with them, smiling while Josh explained the date he had later that night and how the extra money would come in handy. Listening to his hormonal ranting about his girlfriend on the short trip made me miss my youth… and I thought of Matt and I in college.

Knowing what I know now about Matt, would I do it over?

I yelled for Cole to stop the truck, jumped off the trailer, and told him to back up to the big doors while I rolled them open. Josh followed me, guiding Cole back to the door.

I opened the tool box just inside the door, reached for a pair of gloves, and told Josh and his brother to help themselves.

"What are you doing?" Cole asked as I slipped the gloves on my hands.

"Putting gloves on," I frowned at him. I despised mind games, especially sexual ones, but I was having fun playing him.

"But, you don't load hay," he reminded me.

Josh laughed so hard he doubled over.

"What's wrong with you?" Cole asked him.

"You're takin' a real chance with your own life tellin' her that! Shoot, I'm surprised she didn't knock you upside your head with that hay hook!" He chuckled, again, shaking his head. "She put up half this hay last year by herself!" Josh shook his head and grabbed a bale, chucking it on the trailer.

"But, you said…" Cole frowned at me.

"How many?" Josh asked.

"Fifty," I replied to Josh while smiling up at Cole. "You didn't think I wanted to be alone out here with you, with all those bails of hay laying around, did you?" I winked and hefted a bail. "Of course not. So, you're paying for a couple of chaperones." I tossed the bale onto the trailer at Cole's feet for him to stack. Cole pursed his lips and nodded while Josh and his brother turned away their snickering faces. The four of us loaded the fifty bales in a matter of minutes, sweat staining the necks and underarms of our shirts. It would be another warm October day, though it had begun chilly. I wiped my forehead with my sleeve while Cole went to his truck for the cash.

"Here guys. Thanks!" He handed twenty-five dollars to Josh and another twenty-five to his brother. "Here," Cole forced five one hundred dollar bills at me. Josh sat on the edge of the trailer, waiting. Cole stared at him a moment, then turned back to me. "They ride back with the trailer, too." I grinned. "Thank you, sir," I nodded, stepped onto the trailer, and sat crosslegged on the foot and a half of empty space next to Josh, who smiled knowingly at me before shaking his head.

Men! I thought, turning away from Josh as a flush spread up my neck to my cheeks.

The truck bumped slowly to the gate and Josh hopped off; turning back to me, he whispered, "He's a really nice guy. Comes in the feed store all the time." Then Josh opened the gate, walked through, and headed for his truck, little brother in tow. Stopping next to the driver's window of Cole's truck, Josh leaned over and said something to Cole, smiled and turned his truck out the driveway. Was I seriously be match-maked by a teenager? I wondered exactly what Josh had told him about me. There wasn't much for Josh to tell, but still…

The trailer stopped at the edge of my carport, and I eased off, closed the gate, and started the trek toward my house.

"Don't forget about dinner," Cole called, his elbow sticking through the open window of the truck. He winked at me, and I couldn't resist changing my direction.

"You sure you can afford dinner, now?" I prompted.

"Argh, you're right! We might have to go dutch," he answered.

"Well, I have a freezer full of frozen dinners." I shrugged.

"Are you inviting me over?" His brows rose and a twinkle filled his eyes.

"No, I'm saying if I have to pay, then I might as well stay. You asked me out, remember? No, wait, actually, you ordered me to have dinner with you."

"You're the one with five hundred dollars in her pocket!" He pointed out with a crooked smile.

"True, but if you want the date, you're buying." I rolled my eyes and turned toward the house.

He whistled, "Shew! Rich and beautiful," he nodded.

"Oh, far from rich! Are you just going to show up later? Do you want to call me first?" I spun, taking a couple steps backward, then remembered Reba and stopped. I had hoped he would take out his phone to have me enter his number.

"I'll be back around seven." He shook his head as he drove away.

I went in the house, stashed the five hundreds in

the lock box, and returned to my tractor bumping along in the seat to the back pasture where I spent the rest of the day, my silent cell phone tucked into my pocket.

I was running late when I turned the tractor toward the covered equipment barn. Rachel ran up to greet me.

"Are you finished?"

"Yes, ma'am. There will be hay again in the spring." Her eyes lit up.

"Everybody taken care of?" I asked as I climbed down from the seat and dropped to the ground.

"Yep. Can I help make hay this year? You said you would teach me to drive the tractor!" Rachel leaned her back against a post.

"That is up to your parents," I reminded.

"Dang it!" She toe kicked a rock.

"Hey, don't rush it." I pulled my cap off and let my hair loose from its restraint. The chill in the evening breeze forced a shiver after the warm afternoon.

"Oh, they'll never let me drive the tractor!" she

pouted. "I'm lucky they let me ride a horse!"

I smiled at her dramatics. "Well, you are their miracle baby," I reminded, an impish grin filling my face.

"Shut up! Argh!" She crossed her arms before her. I called out to Reba who lagged behind the tractor on the way back. She followed me everywhere on the ranch… perfect guardian and friend.

"How was gramma's?" I asked as I squinted into the falling sun watching Reba's slow return.

"Boring! Are you sending me home already?" She glanced at Reba who broke into a trot when her attention fell on Rachel.

"Well, I kind of... have a date…"

"What? You? Who?" Her blue eyes widened. "You've never been on a date!" she exclaimed.

If she only knew, I smiled sheepishly at her. "Yeah, well," my nose crinkled, "I have ulterior reasons for going on this one."

"Like, business reasons?" Rachel cocked her head and glanced up at me.

"No…" I dragged the word out, "never mix business with pleasure!" I reminded her just before pretending to zip my lip.

"Okay, okay! I'm leaving, but you have to tell me all about it tomorrow! You just have to!" Her ponytail bounced behind her as she and Reba headed toward the fence.

"I do?" I yelled behind her.

"Yes! It's your first date!" I chuckled. My first date? I shook my head. How funny young girls were! I tried to remember if I was like that when I was Rachel's age. I don't even think I liked boys at the age of twelve, just horses.

How could I not have told her about Matt at some point in our time together? "Because you don't talk about your past," I answered myself aloud. But as I pulled my gloves off and tossed them into the tool box, I reminisced over my first date— with Matt.

Art History 101

I glanced at the room number on my course schedule, then at the number on the door. This was it. A little nervous and a little late— I had gone to the wrong building first— I tentatively pushed down on the handle and pulled the door open.

I peeked around the door jamb. The instructor waived me in as she continued her introduction. I could tell then that she would be an instructor I would like. The room was set up like an auditorium with stadium style rows of chairs that included fold up swivel desks. A shrill, catcall whistle came from the rows of students as I entered. With the door still in hand, I turned to look over my shoulder to find the recipient of the call. There was nobody behind me. A quiet rumble of laughter fell from the top row of seats. "Alright, that's enough!" The instructor grinned.

Without disturbing anyone else, or so I thought, I found an empty desk at the front and slipped into it. "She doesn't even know it," a deep whisper came from behind me. Another round of chuckles followed. The instructor kept talking while she dropped a syllabus on my desk, rolled her eyes at the guys above me, and smiled reassuringly at me. I glanced at the daunting 25 page document, thumbing through the pages while I listened. I'd always loved art, but this might be a challenge, I told myself. Leaning forward over the desk, I freed a pen from the side pocket of my bag and began the task of making notes to the syllabus as she lectured.

Thirty minutes later, the instructor released us, and I pulled my schedule out to see when and where I needed to go next. Fortunately, I had a couple of hours to find the building and room, I noted mentally as students around me exited the class. I tucked away my syllabus and pen, took out my campus map, and traced the path from the building I was in now to the building I would go next.

"Hey, that's where I go next!" A guy's voice said as he peeked over my shoulder.

"Well, uhm…" I stammered, having always been a little shy around guys.

"Mind if I walk over with you? There's a courtyard right there!" He pointed at the location on my map with a perfectly manicured index finger. He wasn't into auto mechanics, I noted. "Buy ya' a coffee?"

It was then that I turned my head to look at him. His cheek was so close to mine that my nose bumped it. I leaned away from him. A confident smile lifted one side of his lip while he looked into my eyes. I swallowed hard, stuttering with an apology. "I… uhm… sorry!" I grimaced.

"Yeah, I think you need some coffee." His last word trailed off as his eyes scanned my face before resting on my lips just centimeters from his. A minty scent filled the air around my nose as he spoke drawing my eyes to his perfect white teeth.

I thought he was going to kiss me.

I *wanted* him to kiss me.

I held my breath for what seemed an eternity… waiting for him to kiss me.

His eyes smiled into mine as they met his again, "Yeah, you definitely need a coffee. C'mon!" He took the map from my desk, placed it in my backpack, and zipped my bag before hefting it off the floor near me. After folding down my desk top, he placed his hand on my elbow with a light pressure to guide me into a standing position.

"I'm Matt… the whistler." He introduced himself as he led me out the door.

"I… uhm… I'm…"

"Andi… the one I was whistling at." He stated amused by my puzzled expression. "I saw your name on your schedule, you know… where you crossed out your first name and replaced it with Andi," he added. "Makes it easy for a guy like me to pronounce. It's like you knew this coffee thing would happen." His hand left my elbow and slipped easily to my lower back as he led me out of the building.

"Semester?" He asked.

"Uhm… first, actually." And, those were my very first clear words to him.

"Hey, we have something in common already, it's my first, too— of my fourth year. I put off this art class as long as I could. Boring stuff." He shook his head.

We found a quiet table in the courtyard, and he went to the coffee truck to buy two coffees. I had somewhat recovered from the shock of him before he returned, so we spent the two hours between my classes talking, laughing, and getting to know one another. He walked me to my next class. He'd missed his next class so he could have coffee with me. It wasn't our first date, he kept insisting. Our first date came later that evening, and that was the day, or night, we fell in love— a deeply passionate love that lasted through college and years beyond, but a passionate love that couldn't heal a broken mind.

The following Friday, when I returned to my dorm room after classes, I found a bouquet of wild flowers on my desk stuck haphazardly into a coffee cup filled with water. My phone pinged from inside my backpack, and I dug it out, thinking it was my mother asking about my first week of classes. Unlocking my phone, I quickly touched the message icon.

BTW… I love you.

There was an immediate, urgent knock on my dorm door. Still in shock about the text, I opened the door, and Matt slipped in, locked the door behind him, lifted me off the floor as I wrapped my legs around his waist, and spun me around with my back to the door. He kissed me in a way I had never been kissed, and my body responded. Breathlessly, I whispered into his ear as his lips travelled down my neck, "I love you, too!"

I didn't know where Matt went after we split up, where he was now. I wished I did because he'd been on my mind so much lately. Of course, every time I had the nightmare, Matt was on my mind. I associated him with the accident. My therapist said I didn't blame him, but I blamed the love we had for each other, therefore pushing away any love from my life.

But here I was— years later— thinking of Matt, receiving Matt's text message.

Was he trying to come back to me? Was it possible he changed his number after he left, after I disappeared into my own little world of darkness?

But why wouldn't he just call me?

Had he tried?

Frowning, I walked through my carport and into my kitchen door.

I was about to eliminate one possibility— that someone else learned about our text message, about the accident, about my breakdown, and was using it to send me away again.

But why? Revenge?

The hot shower felt incredible running over my stiff muscles. Throwing hay bales was hard work, though it felt good. I ran a wet, lathered wash cloth over the wiry muscles in my arms.

Farm work kept me in good shape. Of course, it wasn't like I was old or anything. Thirty-two wasn't old. It was old to Rachel, and Josh, but not to me. I didn't feel old. I couldn't believe it had been eight years already since...

No! Stop thinking about it… and about Matt.

I stepped out of the shower and wrapped a towel around my wet hair and a larger towel around my body. The mirror reflected my fogged over image. I looked better tonight than I did that morning when I woke up.

My sticky clean feet patted across the cold flooring and into the closet. What to wear? I guess there was a good reason Rachel thought I'd never been on a date.

How long had it been? *Matt left… when? Two years after the acc… stop!* I mean, I'd gone out a few times with friends but never a date with a man alone, not even a blind date.

Wow, it had been a long time! I really had become a hermit. I wanted to call this a real date, but it wasn't. It was a truth seeking mission.

I had a modest purple dress, and a basic black, but wasn't sure which to wear, or whether to even wear a dress. Maybe he wasn't taking me anyplace fancy. I grinned; after spending so much on hay, it would probably be a fast food joint. I tucked the end of the towel into the wrap at my chest bone and pulled out both dresses, taking them to my room. Standing before the full length mirror on the wall, I held up one dress and then the other. I was leaning toward the black and slid it back over my image, again.

"Definitely black." A familiar male voice whispered after a sharp whistle of approval from the open bedroom door.

I screamed, jumped, and grabbed the towel at my chest, dropping both dresses to the floor in fright. "What are you doing in here? Get out! I locked the door; I know I did!"

"Yeah, I know you did, too." He held up a set of keys, the ring swinging on his index finger.

"You left these in the doorknob. I thought somebody abducted you or something. I did knock!" He grinned at my pink face, I was certain more than my face was pink.

"Wear the sexy black number. It's perfect for where I'm taking you," he nodded, moving into the room to pick it up from the floor.

I couldn't argue with his reasoning on entering the house this time. How stupid! Leaving my keys in the door, I reprimanded myself. It was almost like I meant for this to happen this way. Did I? How could I do such a stupid thing? At least it was Cole who found them. A sigh of relief escaped my lips. And why was I relieved? " I can't believe I did that." I shook my head,"Thanks for checking on me. There's some beer in the fridge, wine on the counter. Help yourself. I'll be ready in fifteen minutes, give or take!" I held the damp towel with both hands, my arms crossed over my chest.

"I'd say... give," His eyes drew almost closed in a squint as he straightened to hand me the dresses. He pulled his lips tight in thought, his head still nodding. He took a step closer, cocking his head to the right, scanning my towel covered body with his eyes.

"No," I shook my head, holding up one finger without removing my hand from the towel wrap. "No, please,… I didn't do it on purpose. Please leave my room now so I can get ready."

I wouldn't allow him control over me like at the barn—not this time— and I was somewhat more helpless in the present situation. He stepped closer, placing his hands up high on either side of the closet door frame. Seeing my chance, I ducked beneath his arm and dodged between his body and the frame, fairly running into the bedroom. Reaching the bedroom door just in time for him to whirl me around to face him.

My hands left the towel to push him away, but in his defense, I did not try very hard. I wanted to feel his arms around me, again. I wasn't afraid of him or what would happen; I was afraid of me. It had been so long since Matt…

And, if this was the only way for me to find out about him, about the sender of those messages…

His hands tightened at my back just as my towel fell and his lips found mine. Gentle kisses on my cheek, my neck, his hands sliding gently around my back, down to my hips sending me into a heated turmoil of passion as he pulled me toward him… and then he pushed away, took a step backward, hands returning to his sides. "Fifteen minutes," His eyes roamed from my face downward, "And, uhm, you lost your towel." He winked, smiling just before he opened the bedroom door, leaving me quivering with desire.

After several deep breaths to calm myself, I was ready in ten minutes, my hair still damp, the purple dress hugging my slender body, no makeup, and a pair of high heels I hadn't worn since Matt left.

"Hmm, that one does actually look better… on the floor, but still good on you." He nodded approval.

"I'm wearing it for me, not for you," I stated, a hint of anger shaking my words.

"Somebody sounds grumpy. Want a beer before we go? Wine?" He opened the fridge and frowned at me. "Maybe a quick spin around the living room?" he turned his smile toward the fridge.

"No, thank you. I'm ready to go, now." *Ready to find out just what the heck is going on and just who you are!* I pouted. It didn't help that he left me slightly frustrated after the bedroom incident.

"You are cute when you pout," he sent a playful half smile my way as his hand found my elbow to guide me toward the door.

"Not my intent!" I frowned again and pulled my elbow free.

"Ow," he held the door open for me, pausing to look into my face. "Is that any way to talk to your date?"

I huffed about that one. Some date! A crazy stalker for all I knew, who was playing mind games— not to mention sex games— with me.

"Where are we going?" I finally spoke after 20 minutes of listening to his truck radio.

"She doth speak," I could see him smiling as he watched the road before the truck hood.

"This is not the way to town," I looked over my shoulder at the left he should have taken toward town.

"Well, not that town," he added. "Don't worry. I'm not abducting you. Remember, I checked to make sure nobody had done that before we left."

"Oh, I feel so much better!" I rolled my eyes toward the darkness outside the passenger window shaking my head.

"Josh was right; you are a feisty one… and cranky. I'm a little disappointed; he didn't say anything about the cranky." He glanced my way, a light grin playing across his face. I turned away, again. *He'd be cranky, too, if he'd been awakened at 3:48 am with a haunting text message, and then left standing naked in his room after innuendos from a seductive temptress. Huh!*

The odd phone number returned to my thoughts, and I focused on their significance. Again, curious about his cell number, I decided to ask him for it.

"*By the way,*" I emphasized the phrase, "what's your cell number?" I pulled my phone from my purse, under the pretense of entering his contact information into my address book.

"Why, are you going to call me after tonight… or, are you premeditating blocking it?" His eyes focused on the farm to market road before us. He was a cautious driver, just like Matt. That was more than I could say for myself. Did he know about my driving?

"Maybe. Depends how the rest of the night goes." I played along.

"Huh, then maybe I'll give it to you before the night is over. Depends how the rest of the night goes," he repeated my comment. A gas station loomed ahead. "I could use some water. Mind if I stop a minute?" he pulled into the lot before I could answer.

"Whatever," I shook my head.

"Want anything?" He asked before closing the door.

"No, thank you." My phone in hand, I wished that I had someone to talk to about this predicament. I'd scrolled through my contacts list, but nobody I could trust with this information caught my attention. Why didn't I have a close friend to talk to?

I locked my phone and stuffed it back in my purse just before it pinged with a text message.

Afraid to take my phone back out— partly for thinking it was *that* text message— I searched the store window for Cole first. All I could see was his cowboy hat and the back of his neck above the shelves, facing a cooler.

Was he looking down? Certainly, he wouldn't be so bold, so evil, as to send me that message while I was with him— would he? I pulled my phone from my purse, hands trembling, and touched my thumb to the home button. My finger hovered, quivering, over the text icon.

Just as Cole opened the driver's door, I touched the icon and let out the breath I'd been holding.

Rachel.

"Everything okay?" he asked, genuinely concerned while he removed his hat, slid the brim between the seat and window, and climbed back into the truck.

"Yes. Everything's fine!" The relief in my words brought a puzzled look from him. I smiled at him, attempting to reassure him, but it felt like a grimace. He had gotten his hair cut sometime this afternoon, and it drew my attention. It was the first time I'd really looked at him since he picked me up, at least without a filter of frustration and anger. His hair no longer hung behind his ears. It was a good cut for him, mussy, sexy, playful.

"Are you checking me out?" He asked, his eyes never leaving the road before us.

My eyes turned downward to the message in my lap.

"How's the date?" Rachel had asked.

I wanted to ignore her, but I was too embarrassed to speak to him at the moment.

"Not so good :- /" I replied. Was that really the truth, though?

"Try to have fun!" She responded.

"K, I will." Huh! Fun?

That was the end of our conversation. Now what? I cleared the message and locked my phone, replacing it in its pocket of my purse.

"Boyfriend?" he asked.

"Yeah. Sure."

"Really?" His eyes widened with a quick glance my

way.

"What? Didn't think to ask that question before now?" I raised my brows.

He smiled. "He coming after me? I mean, just so I'm prepared for the confrontation."

"Yep." I looked out the window into the side mirror at the dark road behind us.

"Okay. I guess if he wants you back, he'll have to fight for you… because at least until then, you're mine. And, you know, I've seen you naked and all."

Oh. My. God. I closed my eyes.

I felt like a teenager. This conversation was stupid. I didn't respond further. I wasn't a doormat.

"Did you sleep okay last night?" His voice had softened and he frowned as he glanced from me to the windshield.

Interesting question coming from him, I thought. Was there a reason he asked?

"Why?" I prodded.

"Well, you seem, I don't know, tense?" Genuine concern filled his face when he glanced my way, again.

Was he serious? He couldn't be, could he? What the heck? I spilled it.

"I had some interesting dreams, to say the least, received a text message at 3:48 this morning and had some difficulty returning to sleep, again, so yes, you could say I slept poorly."

"Oh. I hope it wasn't anything serious!" If he was the sender, he was also a terrific actor.

"What?"

"The text message." He steered the conversation back to the message.

"Oh, it was important all right!" I ended the direction of the conversation with the flat tone.

"Hmm, I turn my phone off at night. I don't want anybody interrupting my sleep." He turned the truck with ease into the right lane to pass a car.

"Really?" I brightened. Maybe he wasn't the one. If that was the case, then who did send the text at that odd time? I relaxed a little. "Can I ask you something?"

"Sure, and maybe I'll answer you," he joked.

"Ha!" I shook my head. *Figures.*

"Seriously, shoot!" He offered.

"Did you really come for hay yesterday?" I studied his face in the darkness.

"Yes, I did." He was being honest as far as I could tell.

"Why didn't you go to the feed store beforehand?"

The truck slowed as we approached Ft. Worth, the city lights brightening the dark highway before us. He took the next exit off the highway and moved to the shoulder of the service lane. He put the truck in park, and turned to look at me. I pressed my back into the passenger door, paranoia stiffening my body. This was it. He was going to kill me and leave me here, on the side of the road in this dark and foreboding area.

Wait! Moments ago, you trusted him. Why would you think that? Your dog trusts him. She loves him. He looked intently across the open space into my eyes.

"Are you afraid of me?" His serious tone confused me.

"No! But, you didn't answer my question."

"I was about to, but you looked so... terrified just now? Look, I went to the feed store, for hay, but they were out. Your little friend down the road, Josh, works there, you know?" Josh had told me he was working part time after he finished with school for the day. "He told me about you. Gave me directions to your house. Told me you were really, well in his words, 'cute for an older lady.' When I saw you working on the tractor, your hair pulled back and tucked under that cap, and then on the horse... I was speechless at how his words underestimated your beauty. I was even nervous." His arm stretched across the back of the seat, hand flipping up in honesty.

"Why'd you leave so suddenly, then?" I prodded.

He chuckled, "I received an urgent text. You were so engrossed in riding, you didn't even notice I was gone. I pointed your buyer and his daughter back to the arena on my way out. Honest."

I wanted so badly to believe him, but I remembered the buyer had said he didn't see anyone, hadn't he? Cole looked innocent, but he had proven himself not so. And then playing those games with me. He was a player. The power he held over my emotions didn't sit well with me. I wasn't used to somebody else controlling my emotions, not since the accident.

"Are we good?" He frowned at me. "If you're still uncomfortable, I'll take you home." He was serious.

Was I uncomfortable? "No way Jack, you owe me dinner! You ordered me on this date." I relaxed into a playful mood.

"Ordered you?"

"Ordered me, yes!"

Laughter shook his chest as his chin met his chest. Looking up again, he turned forward, scanned the mirrors, glanced over his shoulder, and eased the truck back onto the highway. Soon we were back on the highway.

"How much extra did you give him?" I asked.

"Who?" He replied innocently.

"Josh?" I reminded him.

"Huh?"

"When he stopped by your window on his way out. How much extra did you hand him?"

"Oh, I didn't give him anything. He gave me something." He forced his chin forward in concentration.

"My keys?" I raised my brows.

"What? No, I told you. You left those in the door," he reminded.

"Uh, huh. What, then?" *What indeed!* I thought.

"The twenty-five dollars I gave him. He said I would have my hands full with you, and knowing how hard you would be on me, I deserved a break." He pursed his lips as his eyes remained forward.

"He did not!" Now, I was angry.

He turned his seductive gaze my way, his pupils reflecting the highway lights. "Okay," he shrugged.

"Well! You wait till I see him, again!" I shook my head.

Cole laughed in the silence until he guided the truck into the parking lot of what used to be my favorite restaurant.

"Wait, how did you know?" Suspicion filled my mind, again.

"Know what?" He asked as he closed his truck door before moving around to open mine.

"Nothing. I reached for his hand, but he cupped

my waist gently and lifted me out of the truck, closing the door and giving the valet a nod.

The restaurant's dim lighting and gourmet aromas brought a rumble to my stomach as we entered. The host seated us promptly, beckoning a waiter to the table with a wine selection.

Cole ordered a bottle of wine while we searched the menu. By the time the waiter returned, I was ravenous.

"Hungry?" He glanced above the flickering light of the candle toward me. The orange glow danced in his eyes. He was incredibly attractive. A fleeting glimpse of familiarity lay in those blue eyes that I hadn't noticed before that moment. Did I know him? From where?

Sucked in by his eyes, and deeply overwhelmed with the answers to my own questions, I flushed with embarrassment over doubting him. He couldn't be a stalker or some crazed maniac trying to ruin my life! It was just the residual craziness.

"Sorry, I'm staring." He quickly apologized. He reached for his water glass, took a sip, and glanced away.

"No, it's me. I'm the one that should be sorry." Obviously he was a great guy. I was ruining a date with a great guy because of my past, because of a stupid text message.

"You?" His eyebrows rose in shock. "Well, that's an interesting twist!" he smiled.

My face responded timidly. I sipped my wine, its red warmth coating my tongue, my throat, and almost instantly calming my nerves. Over my glass I caught a flicker of intensity in his eyes as he looked across the room.

His smile returned when his focused returned to me.

"Ex girlfriend?" I ventured.

"What?" He removed a breadstick from the basket, took a bite, and chased it down with a sip of wine. I returned my glass to the table.

"Across the room? A girlfriend?" I asked playfully, attempting to lighten his mood.

"What? Oh, over there? No. A business deal gone sour." That peeked my interest. His intense stare, maybe a little pained, bothered me.

My head automatically turned to glance in the direction of Cole's bad business deal, but the light touch of his hand returned my gaze to his. "Don't look, please. I don't want him to see me, get nosy about you."

"Oh, sure, sorry… again." Inside I was dying to look over my shoulder. Time to powder my nose. "That was a long drive. Excuse me?" I watched his face change as his eyes flicked toward the direction behind me and back, again. He seemed nervous, but he smiled.

Was he hiding something from me?

Cole rose from his chair, moving behind me to pull out mine. I wasn't used to this type of chivalry. The waiter offered his help, and I asked directions, quickly disappearing around the high dividing wall. My phone buzzed in my purse. I ignored it as I pushed the door inward and moved to the mirror. Placing my purse on the counter, I glanced at myself, fluffed my hair, pinched my pale cheeks, adjusted my necklace.

My phone buzzed again. "Rachel!" I groaned.

Buzz.

"Damn it!"

Pulling my phone free, I unlocked it and touched the message bubble. There were two. One set was Rachel, the one at the top.

They were the last two messages I received from her with a final smiling emoji.

The other one was from that strange number. The same number that texted me early this morning. 84-384. My finger shook as I touched that message.

BTW… I love you.

"Damn it!" I repeated slamming my phone down on the counter, this time startling a young woman who was just entering the restroom.

"Are you okay?" She touched my shoulder.

"I'm sorry, yes. Thank you. Just an angering message!" I tried to smile at her as I picked up my phone, waving it in her direction and stuffing it back in my purse. I shouldered my bag and sat down on the padded bench, crossing my legs, taking deep breaths, collecting my thoughts. *Text Rachel back so she doesn't worry,* I thought after calming down. Removing my phone, I started to type in "Doing great. Talk tomorrow," but I never pushed the send arrow.

Staring at the odd number, and the personal text message, I convinced myself that it couldn't be Cole sending the messages. I knew it wasn't Matt, either, because… why couldn't it be Matt?

It just couldn't be, that's all! My head shook with the words.

I moved back to Rachel's message and opened it. "Well?" The second one: "how's it going?"

"Fine. Better." I lied.

She sent back another smiley face.

"Are you sure you're okay?" The young woman checked my face from her view in the mirror and then touched up her lipstick.

"Yes thank you. Just… family drama!" I lied, trying to smile.

"Oh, I hate those texts! You seemed to be having such a good time with that amazingly hot guy!" She winked at me. Smiling at my confusion, she added, "We're in the booth to your left. I just happened to notice you two. You make a great couple! Like you are really into each other!"

"Oh, uhm, thanks?" I replied, more a question than statement.

"Don't let the text ruin your night. Turn off your phone. Go have fun. He looks like a keeper. Hang on to him!" She snapped her purse shut and turned to look at me, leaning her rounded hip into the counter. "Good men are hard to find these days."

"You're right." I turned off my phone.

"Well, good. Have a nice evening," she added, touching my shoulder lightly on her way out the door.

"You too," I replied after her. Her kind words, positive, calm thoughts, made me feel so much better about the night. Why let the crazy thoughts, the text worries, ruin an evening of fun? God knows I haven't had fun in a long time! I had the rest of the night to think about those text messages!

My hands steady, I sat for a few more moments of calm, but I couldn't focus on my breathing.

Who was doing this to me? Why?

Was it because I hadn't been punished for the accident? Was it a wife? A girlfriend? A mother? A father? I needed to— wanted to— learn more about the person I hit in the accident. I hadn't needed to know until now. I had felt guilty enough without seeing a face, learning about him or her.

Determined to call the hospital first thing in the morning, I left the ladies room and turned left onto the path back to my table. Over the partition, Matt passed me on the other side, his head tilted slightly downward. He didn't even acknowledge me before he wound around the walkway in the opposite direction. "Matt?" I called after him.

The waiter found me staring after my ex. "Miss,

may I help you find your table? It is this way," and with a gesture of his arm, he led me back to my seat, the seat opposite of my date, who frowned curiously at me—breadstick in mid air— when he saw my face.

My mouth opened, closed, opened, closed.

"You're awfully pale. Are you not feeling well?" Cole leaned in toward me.

I swallowed hard, staring at him as the waiter pulled my chair out. "I... I'm fine. Yeah, sorry, I'm fine. Thank you," I turned to the waiter.

"Your dinner will be out soon. Is there anything else I can get you?" he nodded as he added to wine glass before leaving the table.

Cole frowned at my appearance. "I just... I thought I saw someone I knew." I glanced toward the high dividing wall in the direction of Matt's harried flight.

"From the looks of your face, must have been a ghost from your past. You sure you're okay? Should I whip out my open carry license and go get my gun?"

"Yes!" *A ghost from my past? Did Cole know Matt?* "No! I mean yes I'm fine. No, you don't need to shoot anybody," I nodded vigorously while reaching for my wine glass. It couldn't have been Matt, could it? Was it possible... that they were in this together of some reason, he and Cole? Do I even remember Matt well enough to spot him in a crowd? There were decorative rails from the top of the wall to the ceiling, and just about every man in this place wore a cowboy hat, I noted as I glanced around the room, everyone except Matt. *It couldn't have been Matt. Just a crazy mistake*, I shook my head. Wait! Cole had a gun in his truck?

"I hope you don't mind, but I ordered for you. Steak and lobster tail. You're not a vegetarian, are you?" Cole brought my attention back to the present.

"No, no. I love lobster… and steak. Thank you!" Thinking about the text message, my eyes nervously scanned the table for Cole's phone finding none. I thought again about the person he didn't want to see.

"Are you sure you're okay? It's not too late to cancel the order. If you need me to take you home…" Cole pressed.

"Yes… no, I mean, I'm fine. No, we don't have to leave." I nodded again. I inhaled deeply, exhaled slowly. The scent of grilled steaks wafted in my direction as I did so, causing my stomach to grumble. I needed to relax. If Cole was sending the texts, I needed to know, and if it was Matt and they knew each other, why? It didn't make sense at all. I wasn't going to find out if I lost my mind and left now.

Coles phone wasn't on the table, but somehow I needed to get my hands on it and check. The only way I saw that happening was later, when he took me home. It was a sacrifice I would have to make to gain my sanity, but I had to keep my cool if he was in cahoots with this message business. Fear or anger might send him into a frenzy, maybe even a killing frenzy— if he was a crazy psychopath, that is. The girl in the bathroom didn't seem to think so. She smiled and winked when I turned toward her. I smiled back, stopping my imagination from running wild. I couldn't think thoughts like that, now, not if I wanted to learn the truth. A devious plan took shape while I spoke to him as if nothing had happened.

I didn't understand how or why he or Matt would

torment me with those text messages, though. What was his motive? He seemed like a great guy, the kind of guy I could fall for, and I knew for certain a deep desire for him was bubbling inside me. I tucked my lower lip between my teeth in concentration.

"Did something happen in the restroom? Your mood has changed quite a bit." His question startled me from my thoughts. "No! Oh, no!" I needed to keep my focus in the moment. I tried to smile.

"Hmm… Okay. Have some more wine! Try to relax. It's just a date." He nodded at me while flagging down the waiter with a wave that quickly brought the neatly dressed man to our table to refresh our glasses.

Maybe that was what I needed. To pull this off, a little false courage to calm me down quicker. I sipped from the glass, allowing the warmth of the wine to sooth my tense jaw and throat muscles. One more sip, then another, and…

"Whoa, slow down, there. I'd like you to relax a little, not pass out." Cole chuckled.

"Oh," I laughed. "Sorry, it just… uhm… it's a very nice wine." I held the glass by its stem, turning it slowly in front of the candle flame.

"Ah, a wine connoisseur?" He raised his brows and smiled. "For some reason, I thought you preferred beer." He smiled playfully across the table reminding me of the night before and Reba's treachery.

"No, not really," I felt my body relaxing while my eyes peeked over the glass and took in his strong features highlighted again by the soft flicker of the candle between us.

Returning my gaze, a corner of his lip lifted in

response, his eyes sending a seductive message my way. Later, it said.

I blushed, turning away my gaze to the plate as dinner arrived, and though my hunger had diminished with the wine, I ate, chewing slowly, savoring each bite, and contemplating, trying to pay appropriate attention to him and the conversation. I actually laughed a few times and forgot the messages as though I were on a normal date.

"So, what do you do? I mean… for a living?" I asked curiously.

"Well, I'm the chief editor for a major equine magazine," he replied as he forked a bite of steak.

"Really? Which one?" My enthusiasm increased. Maybe that's where I'd seen him before he showed up at my farm. How long had it been since I flipped through the very magazine that published my articles?

"Oh, that's not important!" He waved away his answer. "I just started, really. I quit my day job to take this editorial position full time."

"Funny, I write for a major equine magazine." My head tilted in question.

"Really?" he nodded. "You know, can we *not* talk about work? I try to keep them separate— work and pleasure that is. After hours is *my* time. What about hobbies? What do you do for fun?" He sipped the beer he'd switched to drinking before dinner was served.

"Fun?" My brows rose in surprise. I thought about that question. "Ride, train horses, teach riders, give riding lessons. To me… I guess that's my fun." I rolled my eyes away trying to remember the last time any part of my life didn't involve horses—the farm— which led me back to Matt.

"We really need to get a hobby," I told Matt as I snuggled onto his shoulder; his damp, bare chest against my cheek.

"We have a hobby!" He replied playfully, placing a light kiss on my forehead.

"Sex is not a hobby!" I laughed, lightly slapping his chest.

"It's not?" I had to raise my head to check his face for sincerity. "Well, how about cycling? We could take our bikes to national parks and lakes, maybe have a picnic?"

"That's a great idea! And perfect exercise! I haven't ridden a bike since I was a teenager. Let's go this weekend!"

"Okay! Then we can load up and find a park to visit on Sunday afternoon. Of course, we'll have to ride until we find a nice secluded location in the park so we can practice our other hobby, too."

"Oh my gosh! I give up with you!" I shook my head as he rolled us over until his face looked down into mine.

"Ah sweet surrender," he whispered before our lips touched.

"Hello? Anybody home?" Cole reached across the table, his light touch on the back of my hand bringing me back to the present. "I'm having a little problem with that candle flame as competition."

The memory left me with a bittersweet smile on my lips, I shook it off as I glanced back at Cole. "I'm so sorry. I just got lost in thought for a moment."

"I would say so. It appears as though I have some competition, besides the candle flame, for your attention. Do I?" He questioned, a frown casting a shadow of concern over his features.

"Excuse me? I mean, no. I was thinking about hobbies actually." It wasn't a lie. "You asked, remember?"

"Oh, well, I hope that one day you look like that when you think about me. Will you take me on as a hobby?" he teased.

A flush crept up my neck into my cheeks as I looked down at my plate. Dead giveaway, dummy! Cole had a skill for catching me off guard. I would have to be really careful. "I'm sorry, hobbies, right?" I glanced across the table after replacing my tripped up tongue with a bite of steak.

"The riding lessons, training, all that, it's not really a hobby? I mean, it's your job, right? Your farm is work. Don't you ever do anything not pertaining to your farm?" The flush returned to my cheeks as Matt flashed into my mind, again. Cole cut a piece of steak and chewed, waiting for my response.

Swallowing, I gave him one. "Not really. I'm kind of hermit to my farm. I stay busy there."

"Hmfph!" He glanced down at his plate and back up into my eyes.

"Well, what do you do for fun?" I turned the focus on him.

"Hmm, I date beautiful women," he joked. "But seriously, I like sports. Do you?" He nodded.

"Yes, sure. Equine sports. Jumping, racing, some rodeo…" A quick thought entered my mind at that moment…"I used to love cycling." I studied his response.

"Cycling? Really?" He seemed surprised. Either he was very good at disguising his motive, or he wasn't the one sending the texts. "Well, bicycles aren't so different from horses, I guess. So for you, everything's horses?" He cast a serious glance my way.

My nearly empty wine glass touched my lips and

the waiter appeared out of nowhere to refill it. Cole waved him off his glass and sipped the coffee he'd requested.

"You're done?" My eyebrows raised in surprise.

"I'm driving. You go ahead. What about dancing? You dance well. Don't you ever go dancing?" He placed his napkin over his plate and the waiter returned to remove it giving Cole room to place his elbows on the table for closer study of me.

"Dancing? No, I haven't been in a long time." Matt was the last person I had danced with, at our best friend's wedding. The memory tried to pull me away from the moment again, back into the past, but I didn't allow it. Vigilance in the present would keep Cole interested, not memories from my past. I needed to keep him interested so I could learn the truth. Not that it was so difficult to stay interested in him. There was something about him…

"Then we'll go dancing!" He smiled at me and leaned back in his chair.

"Tonight?" I pushed my half eaten meal aside, my hunger satiated for the evening.

"Sure. Right now!" He waved the waiter over for the check. Another young man removed my plate. I sipped my wine while Cole took care of the bill. We were receiving the kind of attention that told me Cole was a big tipper, or very well known at this restaurant.

When the waiter returned the leather folder, Cole signed the ticket, stood, pulled out my chair, and offered his elbow, covering my hand with his own.

Giddiness filled my head as we walked to the exit. The electricity crept up from our lightly joined hands and brought my body closer to his. I hadn't been treated like this since, well, never. Did this kind of romance still exist today? I couldn't think of any time in our relationship when Matt pulled out my chair, or took the lead in this way. Oh, Matt was romantic, too, but in his own way and as an equal. We held hands, which seemed juvenile compared to Cole's gestures. Then again, Matt and I were juveniles in college when we met. Based on the attraction I had at the moment, this investigation might turn out to be more beneficial than expected. How long had it been since the last time I'd had…

Mid thought the valet pulled the truck around for Cole and opened my door. Cole placed his hand on my lower back, and guided me into the bench seat. Pushing the door closed, he stepped lightly around the front of the truck, passed a bill to the valet as the attendant opened the driver's door, and then Cole slid into the seat. A smile creased his face when he glanced my way. He seemed really happy.

Was all of the drama— the text message, the doppelgänger— in my head? Was he really just a nice, sweet, romantic guy who wanted to spend time with me? *We have some common ground, and he is very sexy,* I answered my own question.

He drove carefully to The White Elephant, parked the truck, and helped me out, again leading me inside.

"Run a tab?" The bartender called.

"Not tonight, thanks!" Cole replied as he waved to the bartender and led me to the small dance floor.

My face tilted upward to his as he pulled me in close, a slow two-step playing in the background. My hand slid upward over the muscles in his back to his shoulder: his arm lay gently across my shoulders at first, his fingers lightly playing with a curl of my hair. The wine and memories still leading me, my lips closed in on his as he bent to the singular kiss I sought.

When I laid my cheek against his chest, the thump of his heart eased my fears. I felt… oddly safe. The song ended and he twirled me around the floor, moving me away from him during a faster paced song. I don't remember how many songs passed as we glided around the small dance floor. The last song was slow, and Cole pulled me in close again, his hand caressing my back, my upper abs pressed into his lower abs. Desire filled me, a tingle so sudden and deep that I whispered against his lips, "Let's go."

"But we're having a good time. Aren't you having a good time?" His lips touched mine again, and the warm tremors filtering down my spine nearly buckled my knees. "Okay," he agreed when he felt my chest fall against him.

He led me to the truck, guided me into the passenger seat, and I scooted to the middle before digging around for the seat belt. I tugged it across my right shoulder clicking into place. His denim clad leg pressed firmly against my stocking covered one and his knuckles grazed my hip as he set his seat belt. Our legs touching on the ride home intensified our desire for each other.

"Did you move closer, or did my truck shrink?" Cole teased. I smiled in response and rested my hand on his thigh. "Okay, then!" Cole responded, putting his truck in drive and exiting the parking lot, a smile playing across his lips as he tried not to look into my eyes.

"Kiss me, again." I whispered softly against his cheek when he came to a stop light.

"If I do, we won't make it to your house." His eyes remained forward as he exhaled heavily.

"So?" I kissed his cheek lightly, then stroked the hair over his ear.

"So… I'm pretty sure the law frowns upon two naked people in the front seat of a pickup truck blocking a stoplight." He nodded, never turning to face me.

I giggled. "Okay," I said, acquiescing to his implied request.

The drive home seemed much longer than the drive to Fort Worth. The scenic route struggled with the long rested tigress in me and the need to satiate her grew more desperate with each mile. Thoughts tried to surface, thoughts of doubt about Cole, us, the past, but desire forced them back into the darkest recesses of my mind. I would not let the what-ifs ruin what was to come. No nightmares, no texts, no accident. None of that mattered. They were all gone and all that mattered was the here and now, I reminded myself. The fingers on my left hand instinctively caressed his right thigh, again. I felt his back stiffen as he adjusted in his seat. He felt it too, the warmth rising between us.

Arriving at my house, he slipped his truck easily into the space next to my car. Turning off the ignition, he released his seat belt at the same time that I released mine. I felt his hand slip beneath my hair to cradle my neck before he gently turned my head toward him. His lips reached mine hungrily seeking then touching them ever so lightly once, twice, and a third time. Each kiss grew longer than the last and more seeking. Within moments my chest heaved in response. I felt my body easing backward toward the seat, like it had a mind of its own, pulling him downward with me, but he rejected my request and drew back. His index finger touched my protesting lips as he shook his head. Slipping out the driver's side, he stood next to the seat in wait. I slid under the steering wheel toward him, and he wrapped his arms around my waist to kiss me again, a kiss so filled with desire that it made me want to tear his clothes off right then. His hands moved from waist to my thighs then he lifted me from the seat and let my body slide down his until my feet touched the ground. The friction brought a gasp as my dress caught on his belt buckle, removing a layer of clothing from between us. His passionate eyes never leaving mine—he sucked my bottom lip between his own, lingering there, his warm moan of desire weakening my knees.

No words broke the silence as he led me to the porch. I handed him the key and he fumbled with it, trying to unlock the door. Taking his fingers in my own, I pulled the key free and fitted it into the lock with ease, turned it and pushing the door open. His hands rested on my hips as he stepped into the house behind me, then he swung me around, lifted me from the floor and my thighs instantly wrapped around his hips. Our lips opened to each other as he carried me to my bedroom, his hands caressing and massaging the backs of my thighs.

His phone vibrated below my leg, reminding me why I was letting him in. I had been carried away by the romance, but the vibration shocked me out of it. Lifting my mouth from his, I whispered, "Your phone."

"I know." He set my feet on the floor, bending to cover my mouth with his again. Reaching to set my purse on the nightstand, I heard the familiar buzz of a text come from my phone.

A brief moment paused my kiss, but then I thought, Rachel. It couldn't be the message, because he was right here with me.

His phone buzzed against my hip bone as he pressed closer. He dug in his pocket and pulled it free, tossing it on the nightstand next to my purse.

Lost in the moment, we turned our senses to the heated event at hand and left the text messages that followed for another time.

Nothing could stop what was to come. Could one stop a tornado? A hurricane? A beautiful day?

No.

Nothing could come between the nature of our joined bodies.

The tension between us eased after repeated attempts to relieve it, and we finally fell silent. I don't know how much of the night we spent in passionate waves waiting for the tide to subside, but I know how I felt— and that was wonderful! More wonderful than any time spent with Matt. Leaving Matt in the past, I rolled to my side, placing my hand on Cole's chest. My head rested on his damp shoulder and he placed his arm protectively around me with a satisfied, pleasure filled moan. I fell into a contented relaxation that led to a dreamless sleep for the first time in… I didn't know how long.

No tortured nightmares of the accident, no tossing, turning, no unwanted text messages to wake me in the middle of the night.

Just peace.

A spent slumber I had longed for since my life with Matt had ended.

The sun slipped through the blinds and caused an involuntary blink of my eyes. I forced them open with a satisfying stretch, rolled to my back and gently lay my arm out to feel the warm body next to me, but all I felt was a cold pillow. Turning my head, I glanced at the empty space and frowned. Had it all been a dream? I slept too well for it to be a dream.

But where was Cole?

I remembered my purse on the nightstand. His phone had been there, next to my purse. Wherever he was, this was my chance to peek at his text messages.

Surveying the room, the bathroom doors, the open bedroom door, the missing pile of clothes that should have lain next to mine on the floor, I sat up. My dress, hose, heels and unmentionables lay scattered across the room, but no men's clothing could be seen anywhere. His phone was gone, too. Pulling the sheet around me, I stood. Where could he be?

I reached for my purse to withdraw my phone.

Text messages.

Three text messages.

"BTW, I love you"

"BTW, I love you"

"BTW, I love you"

Those unwanted, unnerving, angering text messages!

Growling in frustration, I tossed my phone on the bed and covered my ears, as if that would stop the voices, the torturous words inside promising the onset of another breakdown. The sheet wound around me as I spun a circle near the bed.

Why? Why was he doing this to me?

Who was it? Matt or Cole? Or maybe someone I don't even know? A stalker? But it had to be someone who knew.

Forcing down the nausea that precluded a black out, I stopped, "Deep breaths, in… out," I reminded myself.

My hands pushed upward through my love tangled hair, fingers gently sliding through the mess to caress my scalp as I breathed and then pushed farther up until curls stopped. I gripped the strands at my scalp, and tugged them by the roots.

The tears came, even though I didn't want them.

I couldn't stop them.

The burn of crazy tears stung my eyes.

"Breathe," I whispered more harshly to myself. In… out. Long… deep… breaths.

The tears that only came as I spiraled into a

meltdown threatened to spill down my cheeks.

The stupid, crazy tears!

Get a grip! My mind screamed through the confusion.

It's him, you know it is! He's sending you the texts. This is what you wanted to know! You wanted the truth.

Get a grip!

But was he real? Was he here? Have I already slipped into that made up world?

Breathe… breathe… breathe… breathe… deep… calming… breaths.

Breathe… a sense of calm fluttered in the pit of my stomach forcing back the nausea after several more deep breaths. I blanked my mind of thoughts and pictures, froze the tears in place as they threatened release, and I came through the storm on the other side.

Wiping away the unshed tears with a section of the sheet, I glimpsed my pale face in the mirror.

How much longer must I suffer the torture of near breakdowns?

Breathe, breathe, breathe.

My nerves calmed; I took the sheet with me to the shower to wash away experience. Hot water replaced hot, crazy tears on my oh-so-tired face.

Thirty minutes later, body red from the scalding water, mind fresh from the hot steam, I dressed, made coffee, drank it and moved through my morning routine.

Rachel had not shown, and I wondered why. Walking toward the barn, I paused to take in the pasture, missing Winks and his playful personality.

Something wasn't right, though.

A second horse was missing, too. Who? I counted

again, calling out the names the grazing geldings.

Trooper!

Rachel!

The arena!

A scream pierced the morning, then silence. I ran toward the arena to find Rachel sprawled unnaturally in the sand. Kneeling next to her, I felt for a pulse, listened to her breathing, scrambled for my phone in my back pocket. After dialing 9-1-1, I stayed on the phone until the ambulance arrived, then I called her mother who easily beat the ambulance to the arena. Reba stood watch over Rachel's motionless body and my fragile mind.

"She rode alone. I told her never to ride out here alone!" I cried to her mother. Both hands clasped over her mouth, Rachel's mother ran to her side, dropped to her knees, and sobbed touching her face, cooing to her, begging her to open her eyes.

The EMTs guided the worried mom out of the way, braced the young girl's neck and carefully straightened her limbs. "Watch that arm!" One of them said. After splinting one of Rachel's arms, they rolled her to one side, and slid the board beneath her.

Rachel moaned in reply.

"Rachel. Rachel!" Her mother called, following the EMTs to the now silenced vehicle. "Call Jack! Please…" She begged as the EMT closed the door on Andi's world and sped away.

My eyes searched the arena. In a far corner, Trooper stood quivering, afraid, alone. I dialed the work number for Rachel's dad who immediately left to meet them at the hospital.

The entire time, I moved cautiously toward Trooper, talking quietly to him, calming him. He didn't understand, but then, neither did I. When he stopped quivering, I led him to the barn, removed his gear, and took him to the pasture. I gave him a bucket of grain, just for him. I talked to him, stroked his nose, rubbed his ears. I don't know if he needed it, but I needed it.

I'd forgotten about calling the hospital, forgotten about the text messages, the haunting number, everything.

Rachel was all that mattered to me. Rachel and Trooper. I couldn't recall when Rachel and her family had moved in next door. At the moment, that part of my life was fuzzy. I couldn't even remember when I had moved in here. Was it before or after my accident? Before or after Matt?

Had Matt lived here with me?

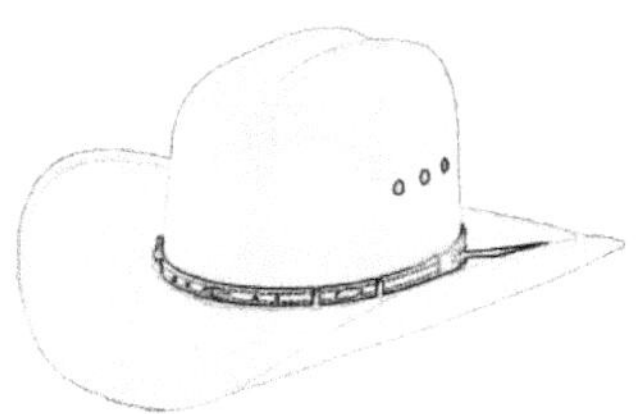

"Andi, you have to snap out of this! This is not you! Since the accident, you haven't been the same!"

"What am I supposed to do, Matt? Tell me! What

would you do if you killed somebody? I was texting you, and I killed somebody on a bicycle!" I screamed at him. I stomped through the house, pacing. But, where was I when I stomped?

"Andi, Andi, breathe. Remember to breathe. It was a freak accident. Nobody's fault! Remember? We don't know the person's condition, but we can find out."

"I don't want to remember! I don't want to know! And it wasn't a freak accident! It was my fault! I was texting you, Matt… you!" But I did stop yelling. I did stop stomping. I did breathe. Matt had reminded me to breathe. For days, Matt was next to me reminding me to breathe. Matt loved me so much. Why couldn't I just let the guilt go and allow us to go back to the way we were before? Matt tried so hard to stay beside me, reminding me to breathe, but the darkness came anyway.

Why did Matt leave?

When did Matt leave?

Why couldn't I remember when I moved here, to this ranch house? I asked myself as Trooper nudged my shoulder with his soft nose.

* * *

Matt's deep brown hair glistened in the sunlight, the white sandy beach such a contrast to his beautifully tanned skin. Muscles rippled around his rib cage.

Matt.

Sneaking peeks at him through the noon sun... watching him watch me... loving Matt. It all started to come back, flooding me with memories of before... Where were we then, the ocean so blue and clear?

Hawaii?

The Bahamas?

His tender touch brought tears to my eyes.

We were so much in love.

"BTW, I love you."

Matt...

Our past, the message, circled me around to the present.

Was Matt sending me those messages? I missed him so very much.

Where was he?

Why did he leave?

When did he leave me?

* * *

"Andi, come on. Don't do this to us. We're supposed to get married, have a family. I love you, Andi. Come on; snap out of it. You're starting to make *me* crazy."

Matt's calm, deep voice filled my mind. I was looking directly at him, but I wasn't seeing him.

I saw the tire.

I saw the text message.

I saw the neighbors pointing their stubby, little, accusing fingers.

I saw guilt.

Red, murderous, crazy tears kind of guilt.

Matt had tears. Soft, loving, gentle tears… just like him.

But it wasn't long before he cried angry, hot tears.

Shame didn't stop him from dripping his tears on my bare feet.

Matt was a loving, sensitive man.

I was going to marry Matt.

He was going to be my family, my only family.

Why did he leave? Why did he give up on me?

Where were we living when he left me? When did he walk out of my life?

Had it all been a dream? Like Cole? Have I always been crazy?

"Andi, you can't expect me to stay around if you're going to remain locked up inside yourself. You have to come out of this. I need you, babe. We're supposed to be getting married, remember?

"Snap out of this craziness that you've wrapped yourself in. Come on, sweetheart…" his soft words, gentle fingers on my cheek, strong arms wrapping me in a tender hug; my head against his strong chest.

Somewhere deep inside, I wanted him to make love to me right then. I wanted that so desperately, but the craziness smothered all emotions, all desires, way deep down inside me, and Matt couldn't reach far enough down to pull back the blanket of guilt.

"Just smile at me, Andi. Just give me that beautiful, wonderful, contagious smile that I fell in love with, that smile that I miss so much."

I wanted to. I wanted to give him that. Matt was my life. He was my world. He was my heart. He deserved that smile.

I wanted to give him everything.

But I couldn't do it.

I tried.

I tried so hard to smile at Matt, but all I could give him were crazy tears. All I could think about was the accident, the guilt. And every time I looked at Matt, I saw the text message, then the tire, then darkness.

I loved you, Matt. Why did you leave me? I snapped out of it after you left. I need you now, Matt. I need you to clear my fuzzy, foggy memories. I need you to tell me where we lived when you left me.

* * *

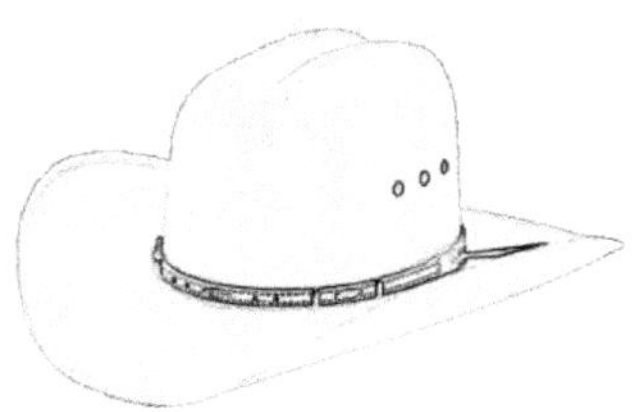

Matt didn't tell me. All I heard was, "I can't do this anymore, Andi. I'm in love with someone else. You remember Elyssa, from the office?"

Which office? The magazine office? Did we work there together—you and me, Matt? Who is she? I don't remember her.

"She knew I was worrying about you. She asked me to go to lunch one day, to talk. We've been going to lunch every day since, like you and I used to do, Andi. I've been seeing her for a couple of years now."

He paused.

I was so angry!

Why would you do that to me, Matt? Oh my God you couldn't wait until… *Until what?* I asked myself.

"I'm sorry, Andi, but, I've tried everything and I can't bring you back to me. You won't come back to me. I did everything the doctor told me to do; I tried. I thought I was the love of your life, thought I could bring you back to us, but I guess I was wrong."

Another long pause. "Remember how much you loved fairytales, Andi? You always dreamed of your prince. You called me your prince. I guess I can't be that for you anymore, because you've shut me out completely. I've tried so hard to bring you back… bring us back. I have to move on."

Another pause.

How long in between pauses?

"Hi, Andi. I wanted to see you one more time. I have something important to tell you. Elyssa and I are getting married next week." I could feel Matt's warm touch as he hugged me, crying lukewarm tears that fell into my hair, slightly dampening the crown of my head as he kissed my forehead, and then he let me go.

Just.

Like.

That.

He turned on his way out, cast a sad smile my way, and said, "BTW, I still love you. I always will."

* * *

"I love you, too, Matt. I just can't be with you right now. I just can't. It was our text. It was us. I may have hit that person, but it was because of you, because of us. You're part of the guilt I will always have. I have to let you go, too."

More crazy tears fell, hot crazy tears that dampened Troopers nose now. Hot crazy tears that gripped my pain filled heart and choked it until the rush of adrenaline slowed, until my heart beat slowed.

But the tears were not the point.

Where did Matt and I live?

Where were we when he left me?

Damn it!

I just couldn't remember!

Trooper moved his nose from beneath my face, then pressed it into the back of my arm and lifted, returning me to the present.

He wanted a hug. He needed a hug.

Or, was it me? Was I the one that needed a hug? Animals were so much more instinctive to the moment.

I'd been leaning into him, my arms draped lazily over the top of his head, scratching gently behind his ears, trying to figure out when I'd moved here, when I met Rachel.

I hugged Trooper, patted his neck reassuringly, just like Rachel did after a bad ride.

"She'll be okay, boy. I wish you could talk. I wish you could tell me what happened."

All past forgotten, I looked into his big, brown eye, my reflection tiny and sad.

Did Trooper see me that way? Tiny and sad?

Had Matt seen me that way? Did Matt see me tiny and sad?

Trooper's eye was sad. I stared deep into his eye until he told me, "Please find out how she's doing, for me."

He wanted me to call the hospital. I had intended to call the hospital about the person on the bicycle. I hadn't called, hadn't wanted to check up on them, since Matt called for me those two times.

"Coma," he told me the year after the accident. "Coma," he told me two months after the accident.

Was that person still in a coma? I wished Matt were here, so he could call for me, so he could find out about Rachel. I hated hospitals.

At the very tender age of sixteen, my older sister died in a hospital. A few years later, my mother went into the hospital and never returned.

That was right after I met Matt in college. Matt had been a godsend. Matt would be my family from then until… Until when? He'd left, but when?

I had never known my father, but Matt had a father, and a mother, and four sisters, and they welcomed me into their family. I longed for that comfort, that camaraderie, but I was afraid. People I loved died. That seemed to be my plight.

I didn't want Matt to die.

* * *

I don't want Rachel to die.

Staring again into that large brown eye, I told Trooper, "I'm sorry, I'm just not ready to call… to check on her. I can't do it. I'm not strong enough." I hugged his neck, again. He stood motionless, his quivering subsided, the fear behind him.

My phone buzzed in my back pocket.

Not now.

I didn't want to look at it—couldn't look at it.

I just couldn't.

I didn't want anyone to love me.

Trooper nudged my arm again as my phone buzzed a second time.

"What if it's bad news?" I lifted my head to look at him.

Buzz. Buzz. Buzz.

I withdrew the phone from my pocket. The screen announced Rachel's mom calling. With dread, I looked at Trooper and then touched 'accept'.

"Andi," her voice cracked with tears. I recognized the sound, that sound of crazy tears. Deafness blocked my hearing. "Andi? Are you there? Come on, Andi! Can you hear me? The doctor's taking her into surgery, Andi... Andi, answer me!" The voice on the other end yelled.

Deafness.

"Andi? Once the surgery's over, there might be a forty-eight hour window of unconsciousness. If she makes it through that, she'll be fine."

Trooper nickered.

Deafness.

No more bad news.

No more crazy tears.

No more text messages.

No more numbers.

No more Matt.

No more Rachel.

No more...

I felt my phone slip from my hand, heard the soft thunk as it hit the grass, the voice calling to me as if it were in a deep well.

"Hello?" Who said that? It was a familiar voice.

"Yes. Uh, huh. I see. I will. Yeah, she's right here, but I think she's in shock."

I recognized that voice, but there was no more caring… not enough to think about the voice. No more.

No more Mom.

No more Sis.

No more...

"Andi? Andi? Come on, Andi. I know you're not that fragile. Don't snap on me! Don't disappear into the shock. Come on." An arm, warm and strong, wrapped a rough blanket around me, squeezed my shoulders, just like I had squeezed Rachel's shoulders yesterday. The arm slipped down from my shoulders to support my back, then found its way under one arm. Another arm lifted the back of my thighs. I was floating. I was nowhere. I levitated, just like the magician at my eighth birthday made his assistant do. It was comforting, like floating in a pool of warm, clear water.

Where did I live on my eighth birthday? Did I have a pool?

"Andi? Come on, Andi, I know you're in there. Come back now. Talk to me." A warm whisper against my ear from somewhere far away.

Where did I live before I lived here… on this farm? Where did I live when the magician floated that girl?

Where did I live when Matt left me?

Questions. More questions. That damn buzzing. That stupid cell phone, buzzing, buzzing, buzzing.

No more BTWs.

No more buzzing.

No more I love you's.

No more…

Deafness.

Darkness.

Where did I live when… Rachel died?

"Andi!"

Somebody voice reached through the darkness toward me. Who was it? Matt?

Someone flipped a switch in the tunnel, a light far away from where I floated in the clear pool.

The voice echoed softly through the immeasurable space and it's soft, warm air tickled my eardrum.

Darkness surrounded me; it was everywhere, the

pin of light grew small again. Then it disappeared, too. No lights broke through the darkness anywhere.

A complete and total black out.

Where was I? Where did I go?

Matt and I took a subway in New York City when we went to that play for our second anniversary… Anniversary? Did we get married?

What was that play?

Why couldn't I remember our wedding?

"Andi!" Louder—the whisper was louder.

Whoever called me was getting closer, but it was so dark in here I couldn't see him.

It had to be Matt. He found me!

Matt!

Matt found me. Relief flooded me.

"Andi!"

That's not Matt's voice.

Who is that? It seems familiar, but who?

Whoever it is, I must thank him for finding me.

Finding me?

Was I lost?

Why did I think that?

"Andi, it's okay, baby."

A soft kiss brushed my forehead. The most wonderful feeling encompassed my cheek, a soft roughness, warm and tender at the same time.

What a nice contrast. Such a wonderful difference. Contrast is beautiful, like the garden bed in front of mine and Matt's home.

With bare hands, I had planted the multitude of flowers, brushing and patting the soil gently over the roots. Such wonderful hues of pinks and purples and blues, with white and yellow scattered among the green foliage as well.

Amazingly comfortable contrasts.

Oh, no! Who's watering my garden?

"Andi? Come on, Andi. You're stronger than this. You have to be. You have to come back to me."

Another kiss, and another on my nose, my cheek, my lips, kisses falling from the sky, landing on my face.

Amazing, how it can rain cats and dogs and kisses. Kisses falling on my garden, the image made me smile.

Kisses falling, falling, falling...

Kisses on my fingers. Kisses on my chin.

Kisses, kisses, kisses...

My life is one big kiss tumbling from the sky above right down on my flower garden.

Sunlight filtered through the blinds.

No, wait!

Car lights, it was car lights.

No, no, it was sunlight. Nobody would drive through a house of kisses.

Nobody, nobody.

Sunlight filtered through the blinds.

Snuggling deeper beneath the covers, I tried to roll to my side, but my body felt heavy.

I didn't want the sunlight—not yet. The darkness was safe, warm, cozy.

Something wonderful made me want to stay right here, right here in bed. A comforting, beautiful, soft, connection stretched the length of my body. I wanted the garden of kisses back in my dreams.

Vaguely, memories of this connected feeling seeped into my broken brain.

A lazy, comfortable smile touched my lips.

I rolled into the warmth, stretching my arms up and over the warm lump next to me.

What was that warm lump?

Wasn't it supposed to be cold like every other morning?

I remember that warm feeling, but from where?

Eyes closed to the light, memories of Matt came and went.

No, silly, Matt's gone. Matt married Elyssa. Matt moved away. Matt couldn't love you anymore. Matt couldn't be here for you anymore.

Reba, then? It must be my Reba. I let her in last night, didn't I? I let her sleep with me.

My hand softly caressed the warmth, embraced it.

Reba's covered with soft white fluff. That's not Reba.

Caress. Caress. Caress the arm.

Horses are much too big to sleep in a bed.

The warm lump moved, rolled, stretched.

"Well, good morning beautiful. Sleep well?"

The light knocked on my eyelids, but I wouldn't open to it. I didn't want to. Matt was gone and there was something not quite right about this voice.

Not quite right, but I smiled.

The light kept knocking... knock.... knock... knock.

"Still sleepy?"

Kiss... kiss... kiss.

The light wasn't knocking; more kisses were falling... falling from heaven onto my eyelids.

"Wake up, Andi. Give me a smile. Give me a pout. Give me a kiss. Give me love. Give me something to tell me you're okay."

That incredible, loving, wonderfully soothing voice. Who was it?

I smiled for him, "I'll give you a smile," I

whispered.

"That's my girl. You're strong, Andi. You can do this."

"Yes, I am… I can." I nodded.

Fingers lifted tendrils of my hair, slipping along their lengths, combing softly. It felt wonderful, that tingling from head to toe. It felt affectionate, intimate. It felt like beautiful, wonderful, love… like kisses falling onto my flower bed, a wonder filled joy crept through me.

Love?

No, that's not right.

I loved Matt.

Matt was gone from my life.

I loved Mom.

Mom has been gone from my life.

I loved Sis.

I always called her. I wanted to call her now and tell her all the great news about Matt and I, about this love I was feeling.

The last time I dialed her number, she didn't answer. It took ten rings before I remembered she'd died.

I loved… What's her name? That girl, that horse girl that comes over all the time…

Oh, yes, Rachel!

I loved Rachel.

I couldn't love anyone else. Not now, not ever. I didn't have it in me anymore. I had no love left to give. This was not love. This was desire, sex, affection, but not love. Who was bringing me those feelings right now?

A strong, soft finger left a tingling trail of affection on my cheek. "I thought you were awake, Andi. Are you dreaming?"

Dreaming? Dreaming of you... maybe this is a dream?

Knock, knock, knock.

Kiss, kiss, kiss.

Peeping through my eyelids, allowing a thin sliver of light to enter, lips loomed large and soft, touching my nose delicately, my lips, my eyelids. Back to my lips, widen the cracks. Let in more light.

Who owns this face behind these gentle lips?

"There you are. I thought you would sleep forever, beautiful!" That deep, spine tingling voice of safety, warmth, love.

That soft kiss on my earlobe. Those strong arms pulling me to him.

Cole. It was Cole!

I remembered.

"Cole? Where did you go last night?" My leaden arms struggled upward toward my head to wipe harshly at the sleepiness on my face, wiping away the tunnel, wiping away the kisses.

This was wrong! Something felt very wrong about the situation, him beside me. Did I have a nightmare? Had he been here this whole time, since our dinner?

I rubbed my ears and wiped away the silence.

"What?" He smiled curiously at me.

"Where did you go? I woke up and you were gone."

"No, Andi. I've been here all along, all night, holding you."

"No. No, you were definitely gone! The sheets were cold. The pillow was cold. Your clothes were gone. I was angry because you left me, but it was okay, because I'd already dealt with those type of feelings when Matt left me, and I survived that. Where did you go?"

"Honey, really. I didn't go anywhere. You're kind of babbling, okay? I don't think you're quite awake, yet. You need coffee. Maybe a hot shower," he winked at me. "Who's Matt?"

"Matt," I closed my eyes to the light, bending my elbow to use my forearm as a shield. Suddenly a fierce headache, a pain so strong pulsed from my eyes, into my brain, through the cracks and down my neck. "Matt, my fiancé. He left me, too." I whispered against the pain.

"Let's move here!" Matt twirled me beneath his upraised arm and drew me to his chest pulling me in tightly. His chin length hair glistened with the heavy dew that had been floating beneath the streetlights on our walk back to the hotel. Looking up into his face, I watched a bead of water drop from his forehead onto mine. He lifted the racing droplet from my skin with his lips spreading a tingle of warmth and safety throughout my face.

"Let's move here after we're married, find jobs, live a life of excitement and fancy restaurants and live plays. Let's move here and make love every night in a studio apartment where we can dance naked in the wide open space. Let's do it, Andi!" A playfully joyous energy lifted his brows and turned up the corners of his lips in expectation as he pressed his slight smile into my own wide grin. Our smiles fell to kisses.

Passion ruled our bodies—passion mingled with wonder, excitement, exploration. Newness led us as we stayed up that night, flowing down a river of passion that struck us each time we spoke of possibilities. We loved each other so much.

We would follow each other to the ends of time.

"Oh, Matt…" I sighed as his warm breath touched my neck.

"Matt again? This Matt was your fiancé, huh? You just called out to him like you would be together forever. Do I have some competition?" The deep voice whispered in my ear, the warm breath bringing me to life.

My hand rubbed at the back of my neck, the pain winning over all else. "Huh? No competition…pain. I have a horrible headache." I rubbed harder, squeezing the back of my neck with my fingers.

"I imagine so. Those were some pretty potent shots. Let me get you something for your headache." The voice trailed off as the motion of the bed brought a cry to my lips.

"No, no, I'll just keep my eyes closed a little longer.

It will go away on its own."

"Well, then let me help you with that." Two fingers gently circled my temples, moved downward to behind my ears, a slight pressure to the motion. The fingers kept moving down the back of my neck slowly massaging the pain away. I relaxed into another deep sleep.

"Andi?" The soft, low voice brought a smile while the moist lips touched my earlobe. "You have to wake up, Andi. Rachel. Remember Rachel? Trooper?"

"The horses!" I sat upright exposing the white lace of my nightgown… part of my wedding night ensemble. When did I unpack this?

Why?

I shook my head— shooting pain.

"No, I have to feed the horses. Oh God, my head!"

"No, the horses have been fed. Josh fed them this morning on his way to work."

"Josh? He's a sweet kid. He's such a big help to me. Rachel helps me, too. Rachel?" My eyes widened with fear.

Full sun, shooting pain, death... "She's dead! Oh my god! I remember! The fall… the ambulance, her mom… oh, no! Trooper! How is Trooper?"

A sigh filled my left ear as a chin rested on my shoulder. I was slipping away again. My head fell back into the softness below. Darkness. "We have to go see her…" breathe in, breath out "…parents." I heard my voice echoing faintly from inside the tunnel.

"Rachel…" Crazy tears flowed from the corners at my closed eyes and into my hair, dew drops tracing my skin.

Warm kisses making them disappear.

"I'll start the shower for you. I'll make the coffee. Time to wake up, Andi. It's time to snap out of this."

"Rachel made me coffee," I answered.

"I know she did. She told me. Wake up, Andi!" The quiet plea trailed toward the bathroom.

Kisses… falling… warm… wet…

Open eyes, open, my brain shouted.

Water…

Hot water, heavy rain falling onto my scalp, covering my quivering body.

I opened my eyes to the drops pounding against my face. My hands rubbed them away and with them the fuzziness left behind by the sedatives.

Reaching around the half glass door of the shower, I pulled my hair towel down, wrapped it around my head, and wrapped my bath towel around my body.

Drops slid down my cheeks, my neck, my spine, my legs. I didn't care. I felt wonderful, alive, in love, like our last night in New York.

A chill touched my skin when I stepped out of the shower, but magically a cup of coffee appeared before me. Who was holding it? Be here now, remember... who?

"It's a little cold in here. You might want to dry off some?" His voice lifted the statement into a question.

"Oh, Cole! Thank you!" Taking the hot coffee, I sipped the liquid, heaven in my mouth, down my throat, into my stomach, waking me up, pushing away the darkness.

Setting the steaming cup on the dresser, I pushed up on my tiptoes and kissed him.

It didn't matter why he left; he was here now... when I needed him most.

Matt had left me when I needed him most.

I know I wouldn't let it go, though. I had to know the truth about the text messages.

Sipping more coffee, I pulled open a dresser drawer, and searched through unmentionables until I found what I wanted.

Cole took the towel from my head and rubbed gently at my hair. Even through the towel, his touch awakened my senses. Tiny puddles formed around my feet as he toweled the water from my hair.

"I forgot to tell you. I had such a good time on our date." My reflection in the dresser mirror cast a joyous smile his way. He smiled back. "Me, too." A glimmer of sadness preceded his downturned gaze and disappeared as quickly.

He wrapped his arms around my toweled waist and leaned into my neck... soft, tingling kisses tracing my shoulder.

My head fell back into his chest and my desire for him grew stronger. I wanted him so badly… needed him so much.

"Come on. You need to get dressed." He patted my hip

A long sigh escaped my lips. I sucked my lower lip between my teeth. "I don't know what to wear."

"Hmm... How about that sexy black number?"

"Of course. That would be perfect for the occasion. Besides, I went against your vote the other night." I shrugged.

In the closet, I reached for my basic, black dress. Every girl needed a basic, black dress, right, Mom? You never knew when you might have to go to a…

My hand paused, eyes focusing on the dress hanging from the padded dress hanger in my hand.

Where would I need a basic, black dress? Why did I have one?

"Andi! You okay in there?" Cole reentered the room with fresh coffee.

"Fine, just deciding."

"What? Your vote is going to overrule mine, again?" Cole smiled from the closet door. "I brought you more coffee. Wear jeans if you want. That might be a little casual for our plans, though."

"Of course! My vote is the only one that counts! I won't wear jeans. That would be ridiculous." A playful smile lit my face as I held the black dress against my body.

Funerals.

That's why I needed a black dress.

I waltzed from the closet, turning, remembering, reliving our date. It was incredible. Spinning into Cole's arms, I whispered, "You're incredible."

"We make a good pair. You're beautiful. I'm incredible." His sea-blue eyes creased with facetiousness.

"You're incredibly handsome. Even in that crisp, black button down and jeans. Will you wear a black cowboy hat?"

"Just for you, darlin'"

"Mhm." I kissed him again, a searching kiss filled with longing.

His hands on my cheeks, he gently pushed me away. "Get dressed, okay? We have to go."

"Okay." He stepped aside, guiding me from the closet. How he'd changed since spending the night.

Holding out the black dress, eyeing it for wrinkles, my smile fell.

Black.

Black was for funerals.

I wore a black dress to Sis's funeral... was it *this* dress?

And Mom's funeral...

So, of course, I would wear one to Rachel's funeral. I scanned the dress, again. "Oh! I can't wear this, Cole! Look! There's a stain!"

Cole took the hanger from me, held the dress to the light, and squinted, "Where? How can you see a stain on a black dress?" He shook his head.

"Right there," I drew a circle with my finger around a dark spot on the skirt.

"Andi, there's no stain on this dress." His brows drew downward in concern.

"There isn't?" Squinting, holding it to the light of the window, I discovered he was right. There was no stain. Why had I thought there was a stain?

After slipping into my hose, my dress and my heels, I picked up my black, leather purse and transferred everything from my everyday purse into it. My phone eluded me in the mess, until the very last. I held it in my hand, the screen dark. I pushed the button on the top. Nothing happened.

"I can't go. My phone's dead. I need to charge it." I shrugged.

"Andi, I have a charger in the truck. Now, if I have to carry you I will, but we are leaving right now. You've been stalling since you woke up and I can't for the life of me figure out why." He tilted my chin upward to better check my eyes.

A sigh, a pout but nothing worked. He placed his hands on my shoulders, spun me around facing the door, and lightly guided me through the kitchen.

"Are you sure Josh is taking care of everything?"

"Yes, Andi. You know him. You know he's responsible." Matt lifted his black felt hat off the kitchen island and placed it on his head with one hand, keeping the other firmly planted on my shoulder.

"I know he is. I just worry about them… my horses." The carport door loomed before me. Cole's hand reached around me, turned the knob, and tugged it open.

"Horses have been taking care of themselves for thousands of years, Andi. They'll survive one day without you."

So this was it, then? I asked myself.

This was it, I replied. My head nodded as I a forced confidence straightened my spine.

One step into the cool morning air. At least the sun

was hidden behind clouds.

My heels clacked on the porch. I did it. With Cole's help, I did it. I left the house.

"I'm doing well," I smiled. A wisp of drizzle touched my face. It was going to rain.

"You're doing exceptionally well!" Cole humored me, kissed the crown of my head, his hands guiding my shoulders, my heels clicking on the concrete pad.

Reba licked my fingertips. She knew when I wore black not to rub against me.

Black and white. How funny!

The world was not black and white. It was much more complicated than that.

But today, the world was black.

Cole held open the passenger door of my SUV and sat down, pulled in my feet, and closed the door.

"It's nice to take my car sometimes." I smiled while he adjusted the seat, the mirrors, the steering wheel. He was a careful driver. I was glad of that. I didn't mind him driving me anywhere.

"It's such a dreary day. I really hate to get all dressed up and go out on days like this." I checked under the seat for my umbrella.

Cole frowned at my comments. Then he chuckled, his chest shaking, and shook his head.

"What? What's so funny?"

"You. You're so dramatic today! I would have never guessed when I first met you." He shook his head, looked over his shoulder, and backed into the driveway. He was so careful.

He wouldn't text and drive.

He wouldn't hit a bicycler!

"No, I'm not dramatic. Rachel's dramatic! Have you met Ra...?" My eyes rolled to the gray clouds outside my window.

"Andi, do you know where we're going?" Concern clouded Cole's features.

"Yes, but I really don't want to go. It's so dreary, sad, depressing. Funerals are depressing."

"Ah," another chuckle, another shake of his head. "The doctor said you would be fuzzy for a while."

"I'm not fuzzy!" I looked down at my black dress misunderstanding his meaning.

"Not your dress, your brain," he clarified.

"Do we have to go?" I sighed and turned toward him.

"Yes. You need to see Rachel. You told her parents you would be there."

"I'd rather not. Actually, I don't want to... I don't want to... remember her like she was that day... that day I found Trooper quivering all over from fear... that day... was horrible." I returned my gaze to the cloud darkened world outside my window.

"What? Andi, stay with me, okay. Your eyes are glassing over, again. Come out of the fuzz! Drink your coffee," a nod, a squeeze of my shoulder, strong fingers. I needed strength today… so much strength.

Lifeless clouds, drizzle dancing against the window, just the type of droplets that made a mess of the windshield when wiped away. My vision blurred as I stared out the windshield.

No! No crazy tears! Not today! Today was special. Today was...

Rachel's funeral.

"Why are you wearing that to work?" Matt eyed me as I tried to pull on my high heels one at a time between steps down the hallway.

"What's wrong with it?" I scanned the front of my dress before reaching for my travel mug.

"Nothing… it just…" he paused, brows furrowed

disapprovingly. "It just looks like you're going to a funeral."

"What?" My tone rose in a crescendo of humor.

"So, now you're laughing about funerals?" Matt scowled.

"Well, no, I'm not laughing about anything. What's wrong with you this morning?" I moved toward him and reached a hand up to comb my fingers through his hair.

"Nothing's wrong with me!" He defended, dodging my hand and pushing my arm away. "Go change. I'm not dropping you off at the office with that outfit on."

"What? Matt?" He wouldn't even look at me, wouldn't discuss it. "Well, if it bothers you that much, I'll change. We're going to be late, though."

"What difference does that make? You always make us late," he mumbled. The words still stung as I returned to the bedroom to find a different outfit.

We didn't speak on the way to work. Matt wouldn't even look at me when he dropped me off—one rolling stone in the avalanche that would soon crumble the power couple dream.

"Andi? Don't do this to me… to Rachel."

Matt? My eyes closed tightly against the tears, against Matt's voice calling me out of the darkness.

Matt left you, idiot! Get over it! I screamed quietly at myself.

Fluttering eyelids, my vision refocused on the end of my driveway. My head turned right, left, right again. I reached for my phone to plug it in. We eased out onto the road.

The tire rolled into my peripheral vision.

No! Not that damn tire! Not again! I pressed my palms to my temples to squeeze away the memory.

"Andi? Come on. Focus. Stay clear headed." The car braked just before strong fingers pulled my palms away and caressed my cheek. The fingertips turned my chin toward him and he gently kissed my lips, "Do you know where we're going?" His eyes dimmed with concern, his brows furrowed, his lips brushed mine again.

Cole.

"Yes, yes I know where we're going."

"That's my girl. Stay with me. Stay right here beside me, *mind* and body."

My lips whispered, "I will," followed by a nod, but could I really? Did I have control over my own faculties? Could I stay with him?

Of course not!

I was crazy!

"I forgot. Where are we going?"

"To see Rachel."

"I don't want to see Rachel." I shook my head frantically.

"Well, she wants you there. She specifically told her mother that she wants you there. She asked if Trooper could come, too, but her mom nixed that."

"What are you talking about? Who's the crazy one now?" I rolled my eyes.

"Who said you were crazy? Nobody said anything about crazy. A little stressed, a little shocked maybe, but not crazy." Cole's head bent forward and turned slightly to study my face.

"I am, though. I've lost it completely. I lost it the day Rachel died. I've cracked. I've had enough of death. You may as well leave, too, like Matt did. I can take it. Really!" I argued with the windshield.

"Matt again? Really, Andi? And I'm not going anywhere. I'm not leaving you. We're going to see Rachel." Cole's sympathetic tone turned sad as he struggled to make me understand something, but what?

"You did leave me. After our date, the next morning you were gone. And you might be better off leaving me now. Today after the funeral..." Tears puddled in my lower lids.

Cole chuckled. "Oh, I understand now."

"Oh, so now you find funerals funny?" The tears overflowed and spilled down my cheeks.

"What? Andi, do you know how long it's been since the accident?" Cole's fingers combed a curl behind my ear. I wanted to slap his hand away, but why? He was so good to me.

I snickered, and sniffled, and the crazy tears came again, "Eight years, four months, and three days." I closed my eyes against the burn.

"What? Where did that come from? It's been a week. One week. Seven days. You've been in shock, in and out. I've been with you the entire week." Cole placed his hand on the back of my head, massaging my scalp lightly.

"No, you're wrong! You left me once! And it would probably be better for you if you left, again." I rotated my neck to move away from his touch and watched the water drops forming on the foggy exterior of the passenger window.

Drab day for a funeral.

Perfect day for a funeral.

Ideal outfit for a funeral.

"Andi, I'm not leaving. I left after our date because of a text message I received. I came back the next morning and found you with Trooper, both of you in shock. Rachel's fine, Andi. The Vet came out and took care of Trooper. Rachel's just banged up a little. We're not going to her funeral. I promise." He eyed me before easing back out onto the road.

My head tilted to his voice. I frowned. No funeral?

"Then why are we wearing black?" I vocalized curiously.

"After we go to the hospital to see Rachel, we're going to the award ceremony. When I asked you yesterday, you said yes, you wanted to come with me." He kept his eyes on the slippery black top ahead as he spoke softly.

"Well, I don't want to go!" I paused, lowering my

voice. "Rachel's really okay?" The words sounded so small, like a tiny child asking a parent a delicate question.

"Yes, Andi. Rachel's coming home today. She has a broken arm, but she's okay. And we don't have to go to the award ceremony if you don't want to. What's another journalism award?" Eyes never leaving the road in front of him, he reached over and took my hand in his.

Relieved, my heavy lids fell closed, again. I pressed back into the headrest. Breathe deeply, in and out. Relaxation filled my body with the tenth breath.

"Better now?" Cole guided my hand to the seat between us and gave it a gentle squeeze.

"Yes, and even more so when I see Rachel. I think my head's clearing." I chuckled lightly.

"We'll be at the hospital soon." His thumb caressed the knuckles on my hand.

"So you got an urgent text message? That's why you left after our date?" My thoughts clearing, I remembered his words. Remembered why we were together, my plan to find out if it was him, the haunting texts.

"We don't have to talk about that now, do we?" He pursed his lips in denial.

"Of course, we do! It's been bugging me for days! I

thought you were like… like Matt." I struggled with the last two words, something deep inside telling me not to bring Matt up again. I was pushing for an argument, but I didn't know why.

"Well, I'm not!" He gave me what I wanted, a tone I hadn't heard him use yet and he removed his hand from mine, placing it back on the steering wheel—ten and two.

"I know. You're a wonderful man who will always be here for me!" The remark came out snide, but I meant it, I thought.

"You're still not back to normal. It's the sedatives. They'll wear off soon." He took a deep breath, the red draining from his face.

"Before the hospital?" I hoped. I didn't want Rachel to see me this way.

"Sure, I guess." He sighed, frustration filling his words.

"The text? I've been getting text messages, too. I thought you were sending them, but it can't be you. You love me."

"You heard *that* part, did you? Well, yes. I know it seems soon, but I do love you. Believe me, nobody's as shocked as I am," he looked surprised. "Since the first time I saw you with that streak of grease on your cheek. What kind of text messages have you been getting?" His hand pulled mine back to the console between us. He caressed the back of my hand with his thumb.

"The same message I sent right before the…" He didn't know about the accident— or did he?

"The what?"

"The accident. When I hit the bicycle. Somebody's been tormenting me with the text message I sent Matt. I think somebody's mad because I didn't get charged for texting while driving." I turned to him, relief filling me as I finally spoke the thoughts aloud.

"Come on, Andi. You know how that sounds, right? Surely, that's not true. Who would do such a thing?" He shrugged in question. *Could I trust him?* I was divulging my secrets as if I could.

"Well, I thought it was you. The messages started the day you showed up at my place. It has to be real. I'll show you when my phone's charged."

Those catching blue eyes threw a suspicious glance my way. He believed me, didn't he? Did he know something about the messages? Cole's quick look away led me to believe he was hiding something.

"I was going to check your phone the night you slipped out. I was going to wake up in the middle of the night and check your phone to see if you sent me those messages," I admitted.

Was he offended by my plan? No, no that was

definitely anger, wasn't it? He glanced my way like he wanted to slap me.

"Did you? Did you look at my phone, Andi? I mean, that's kind of invasion of privacy!" His harsh words created a rush of embarrassment in me, but my courage built against his words.

"Why? Are you hiding something from me? What if I did look?" He inhaled through his nose, filling his chest with a relaxing breath, then exhaled through his mouth, bringing a calm, releasing his frustration. "What's your phone number? You never gave me your number," I responded.

"Andi, we're here. Look," he nodded toward the tall building beyond the windshield. The parking garage of the Children's Hospital looming before us. "We'll finish this conversation later."

"You always find a way to evade my questions! Why won't you just answer me? Let me see your phone! Now!" My face paled with suspicion.

His eyes closed, opened, then the light changed and his features shaded over as we entered the dim lighting of the parking garage.

Darkness filled the car, followed by brief flashes of light as Cole followed the arrows to the right floor, turned into a parking spot, pushed the button on the shifter to park, and turned off the ignition. He turned in the darkness, reaching toward me with his hands.

"Don't touch me!" I pressed my body into the door behind me. His hands fell to his lap and he faced the concrete pillar in front of us.

"Andi. We're here to help Rachel. She wants to see you, and she doesn't want to see you like this." He turned toward me again, reached out and cupped my face in his hands. His palms felt warm on my cheeks. "Come on, Andi," he frowned sadly in the darkness. His weary face pled with me to listen and I suddenly realized how tired he looked. A week with me? Taking care of me?

"You'll give me your number later?" I pouted.

"To prove that I didn't send the messages? Is that what you really believe? My word isn't enough?" His features softened as his thumbs gently stroked my cheeks.

"Because of the text messages, yes. I have to know that it wasn't you." My eyes closed to his tender touch.

"Okay, later. Rachel's waiting. She's being released any minute." He exited through the driver door and walked around to open my door. I stepped onto the concrete, the parking garage a dim tunnel. He led me by the elbow to the entrance.

Would I ever be sane, again? Had I ever been sane? "You promise?" I hesitated.

"Yes, Andi, I promise. If it will make you happy, I

promise." The glass doors swished open as we approached. We turned down a long hallway, following the signs for the elevators. Cole pushed the elevator button, then pulled me into his side planting a reassuring kiss in my hair before we entered the small space.

The steel doors whooshed closed. I stepped closer to the rail and leaned into it, Cole's hand on the small of my back. I frowned as I felt more clarity wash away the fog.

Over my shoulder, I searched his face. He saw it, the clear look in my eyes, and smiled. "You're back, again, huh? Feeling a little better?"

"What happened? Why do I feel so strange, like I've been dreaming forever?" Puzzled by the many questions floating through my mind, I shook my head again.

"Well, first, you kind of lost it when you saw Rachel lying on the ground. Then..." he replied playfully.

"Oh, yeah, Rachel!" I watched the signs indicating the floor numbers as the light of the buttons rose with each ping. "What floor is she on?"

"Eight." He squeezed my shoulders, a happy to see me kind of squeeze.

Deep breath in, slow exhale out.

In and out, I reminded as lighted numbers began

to catch my attention.

3.

4.

8... No, no, that's 5!

3.

4.

8.

Breathe in, exhale. That's right, I told myself. Keep it together.

Ping! Another red button on the wall, another set of doors gaping toward us.

Cole's arm remained firm around my shoulders.

Click, click, my heels tapped lightly on the tiles.

Cole tugged on my waist, spinning me toward him as he backed into a vending machine alcove, holding me tightly against him, spreading a warmth of desire throughout my body, "You sure you're okay, Andi?"

"Yes. Yes, I'm fine, now. Crazy, right?" I nodded, searching for onlookers who may be eyeing what might seem inappropriate behavior for a hospital.

"Are you sure?" He squinted, lifting my chin, studying my eyes.

"Yes. Yes, I'm sure," I nodded, again.

"Not everybody dies in hospitals, you know, Andi?"
Why would Cole say that?

"Of course not. Of course not!" My head shook. I

felt my shoulders rise and fall in agreement.

His eyes crinkled. He tilted my face up to his, "I'm glad you're back. Come on." He turned me around by my shoulder and pulled me close to his side as we walked.

"Wait was I gone somewhere?" I joked.

"Just for a few days. After the accident, then on and off since, but that's not important. You're back. That's the important part!"

"Yes, of course! Rachel's down here, right?" He nodded as we moved down the hallway.

"Mhm," he nodded. "Room eight forty-three, right down this way, according to the signs." My knees buckled. Cole held me up by my waist.

Room 843!

Those numbers, again. Those damn numbers. The text, the numbers, the...

Like someone pulling a pistol trigger, the numbers set my thoughts spinning.

No!

In and out. Just breathe.

843.

Just breathe.

Cole pushed open the room door.

I swallowed hard.

One step.

Another step.
Click.
Click.
No carpet.

"**A**ndi!" Rachel sat on the side of the bed smiling. "Oh my gawd! Look at you!" Rachel exclaimed when we walked in. "Be the first one to sign my cast, please!" Her thrill over having the plaster protection from hand to elbow made me smile.

"Sure. Absolutely! Even though you broke the rules!" I sent a reprimanding look her way.

"Rachel, really! Andi just got here. Don't be so impatient! How are you, Andi? You look amazing! That dress is perfect for you." Rachel's mom moved close to me and touched my arm with a look of confidentiality.

"Oh, thank you. We have a thing later. I'm great! How are you?" I sputtered, acting as if nothing had happened.

"Better, now that this is about to be behind us. I don't think Rachel will be riding for a while, though," Rachel's mom looked up at Cole, passing a questioning look to him. A slight nod of his head, and then she hugged me. "I'm glad you're okay, now," she whispered in my ear.

I squeezed her back, then moved to the side of Rachel's bed. "So, no riding, huh? You won't be much help to me with that broken arm, either," I tightened my lips disapprovingly.

"Uh, Mom! The doctor said I could do whatever I could do! I can ride with one arm, and I can feed with one arm!" Rachel's eyes widened at me.

I hugged her. I'd missed her spunkiness. Trooper missed her, too.

"Hey, Trooper misses you!" I tapped gently on the cast.

"Ugh! I can't wait to get out of here! I want to see him. Is he okay?" She frowned. Just like her to worry about him instead of herself.

"Yep. He's just fine. Back to his old self, right Cole?" My head bobbed as my eyes scanned from Cole's belt buckle, up his black shirted, strong chest, to his clean cut features where I found his return smile sealed with a wink. "Yep! He's doing fine."

"Hey, you got out of telling me about your date! Is this the guy? He's cute for an old guy!" Rachel leaned in to whisper in my ear.

"Rachel!" Her mother scolded.

"Well, you know, it wasn't my fault. I came out to tell you all about it, but somebody decided to break my number one rule…" My lips tightened in disagreement, and I looked up at the ceiling.

"Wait! You were going to tell this *young* lady about our date?" Cole feigned surprise.

"Why did you say it like that?" Rachel confronted Cole. "Why did he say it like that?" She turned to me. "Whatever, I'm twelve! And anyway, I'm supposed to break the rules! I'm a kid."

"Uh, no young lady, you're not supposed to break the rules!" Her mother offered over my shoulder. Cole and I laughed at the bantering and when I looked at him, I found a look of relief in his face that made me smile.

The nurse wheeled in Rachel's ride to the car, "Okay, young lady, time to bust outta here!" She added as if Rachel had been imprisoned.

"What's that? I don't need that thing! I didn't break my leg!" Rachel smarted.

"House rules. Let's go!" The nurse pointed to the seat.

"More rules! Is that all adults do, make rules?" Rachel plopped into the chair.

"Yes, that's what we do. Feet up, please!" The nurse smiled and shook her head.

"May I?" I stood, taking the handles of the chair from the nurse.

"Sure!" She bent to release the brakes. "I've had enough to do with this drama queen!" She rolled her eyes teasingly toward Rachel as she straightened up.

"I'm not a drama queen!" Rachel whined.

We all laughed as I pushed Rachel down the hallway.

"We'll go to the elevators to get to the first floor. If you parked in the garage, you'll have to bring the car down to the pick up area." The nurse instructed Cole.

I was back.

Rachel was okay.

I was okay.

Wasn't I?

"Okay, I'll go bring the car around," Cole separated from the group to exit the same way we entered.

"It's nice of you two to come get us," Rachel's mom said as the elevator doors closed.

"Well, I kind of feel responsible. I mean…" I shrugged at her.

"It wasn't your fault, Andi. It was my fault," Rachel sighed.

The elevator doors whooshed closed.

8…

4…

3…

"Stop!" Suddenly I needed out of the elevator. Something wasn't right… a memory? I shook my head.

The elevator stopped.

"Where are you going?" Rachel whined as I moved past her wheelchair.

"It's okay. You go meet Cole at patient pick up. I'll be down in a few minutes. I have to check on someone!"

"What? Who?" Rachel asked her mom who shrugged her shoulders in reply as the doors slid closed.

* * *

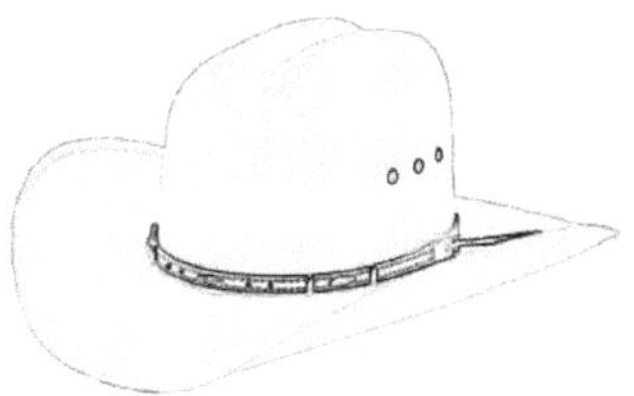

"You don't need to go to the hospital, Andi. Just let it be!"

I returned the car keys to the holder next to the garage entrance. "I have to do something. I'm losing my mind with worry. What have I done, Matt? I need to know!" I pressed my forehead into the door frame as the tears came again.

"Andi, it was just a freak accident. Let it go. You're still in shock. Why don't you go back to bed… try to rest?"

"I'm tired of being in bed, Matt! I'm tired of resting! I'm tired of medication!" I shouted. We didn't yell at each other. Immediate remorse for raising my voice sent me down the hallway, back to our bedroom.

Matt followed close behind. "Don't you ever raise your voice to me, again! I don't care what you're going through. I didn't do this!" He gripped my shoulder a little too hard and spun me around to face him. "Listen to me, and hear what I am saying. I have to go into the office. Do not leave this house! We don't know what kind of trouble is going to come out of this, Andi. We haven't heard anything. Stay home! Do you understand me?"

His grip tightened and he shook me for emphasis.

"Ow! Okay. You don't have to inflict physical pain. The emotional pain is enough." I turned away from him.

"I'm sorry. God, Andi, I'm so sorry. I didn't mean to…" he pulled me into his arms. "You can be so stubborn. I just… I'm sorry."

Nothing would be the same for us. I knew it then. I stayed, though, didn't I? I stayed home that day, and the next day, and the next…

When did I return to work?

Passing the nurse's station, my heels clicked on the tiled floor presenting an eerie sound down the long, empty corridor. Suddenly, I felt very alone in this hospital. My vision so focused on the room signs as I passed that I couldn't see the well lit way before me.

Now which hallway is it?

I should ask.

Ask for whom? I never discovered who was on the bicycle.

No, I don't need to ask. I remember which room they are in.

Why would I remember that? It's obvious, isn't it?

I'll just stop in and see if they're still here. Who? How would you know who he or she is? You never got to come to the hospital, connect with the family. Matt wouldn't allow it.

My feet stopped at the intersecting hallway while I continued the absurd, silent conversation with myself.

I looked right, left, right and stepped out… to the left following my instincts.

Which door was it?

My feet led my mind, down the hallway, door… another door… and another.

Moaning to my left.

Crying to my right.

Beeping, beeping, buzz, buzz. The sounds in the hallway were starting to distract me.

Where were the nurses? Why was it so dark?

Buzz.

Buzz.

Buzz.

What is that noise? I paused midway down the hall.

Oh, my cellphone! I dug around in my purse. I didn't have to! I knew what it said. I knew it because…

The corner of my phone pinched between thumb and index finger, I dropped it back into my bag.

Focusing on the click of my heels as I moved down the hallway, the subtle insanity left behind by the multiple machines in the rooms seemed long gone.

I stopped me in front of a large, plate glass window. The blinds were closed.

Placing my hand on the door next to it, I gently pushed it open.

Someone was in the bed. Hoses, tubes, machines filled the tiny room.

Beep.

Beep.

Beep.

Buzz.

Buzz.

Who was that in the bed? It was a man, wasn't it?

From my angle, I couldn't tell for sure, but did he resemble…

Buzz.

Buzz.

"Shut up!" I whispered harshly toward my phone so as not to disturb the person lying in the bed. Could I disturb them?

Buzz.

Buzz.

Why? Why was this stranger sending me these text messages? Who would torture a person like that? Even as angry as Matt was sometimes, he wouldn't be… he couldn't be!

Why did I say Matt was angry? He was never angry. We had a perfect life… the power couple in love. Matt would never torture me like this. It had to be…

I reached into my bag, my resolve overcoming this stalking intrusion in my life. I decided I was going to text the person back and ask who it was. I'd had enough! This entire week had been some kind of hell.

The person in the bed—his face turned away from my view—moaned. Looking up from my purse, I glanced toward him, his hair so familiar. I took a step forward to get a better look at his face.

A strong hand gripped my shoulder and my phone clattered to the floor.

"Andi? What are you doing in here?" A whisper of words fell to my ear.

"Looking for my cell phone!" My hands rummaged through my purse as the room door fell closed behind us.

"It's in the car. On the charger. Remember?" Then what fell from my hand?

I smacked my palm against my forehead. "I forgot!"

Buzz.

Buzz.

"Who's that?" Cole nodded toward the patient's lying in the bed.

"Well, it's…" I looked up at the body covered with white sheets, a thin blanket, tubes and cords flowing from him in every direction. The old man lying in the bed, his face now turned toward me, eyes barely open from our intrusion, hair white as snow.

"...I ...I don't know." I searched the floor for the item I dropped from my purse, but there was nothing. Then I saw the corded remote lying near the hospital bed.

Cole took me by the elbow to guide me from the room and back to the elevators, "Wait!" I moved to the bedside and replaced the remote next to the man who now looked me, a faint smile on his lips. He was so frail and his words of gratitude more so.

A nurse pushing a wheelchair passed us in the hallway. I watched over my shoulder as she wheeled the elderly woman to the end of the hall, the octogenarian's moans muffled as they moved farther away.

An orderly guided an empty roller bed around us and into the elevator next to us.

"Are they in the car?" I turned to Cole as the doors slid open.

"Yes, they've been waiting for a while. They told me you had to see somebody. Did you?" He slipped his arm around my waist in a gesture of comfort.

Cole pushed the ground floor button with his free hand.

"No, I was going to check on someone..." I shrugged. "...but, I couldn't find him ...or her?" I frowned, thinking.

Cole studied my face curiously.

"Who?" Cole asked as the elevator bumped downward.

"Well, I don't really know. I didn't want to know before. Now, I think I do want to know. I *need* to know, so I can let go— move on." I nodded.

"Are you sure you want to do that? Find out? Now?" He bent his head to better view my face.

"You're right. It's probably not a good idea to keep Rachel and her mom waiting anyway. Rachel's anxious to see Trooper."

"Very! You should have heard her in the car before I came back in to find you!" Cole perked up.

I laughed. That's Rachel!

The elevator opened to the ground floor and Cole led me to the patient pick up door. Opening the passenger door, he held his hand out to help me step in, then closed the door and moved around the back of the car to the driver's side.

"Such a gentlemen!" Rachel's mom whispered before he slid into the seat.

My eyes watched the hospital get smaller in the side mirror as we left the parking lot.

I did it.

I went into a hospital.

Everything was fine. Rachel went in. Rachel came out. She was fine, other than her broken arm. I could now return to a normal life. I guess it was for the best that I didn't find who I'd hit. I mean, certainly the person was out of the hospital by now. What a moment of crazy thinking that old man was…! Who?

I reached across the console and took Cole's hand. It was so strong. I needed his strength now.

"Yoooo!" Rachel mocked.

"Hush!" her mother scolded.

"Andi and Cole, sitting in a tree…"

I laughed. She was so young.

"Rachel! I'm warning you!" Her mother said, her

voice threateningly quiet.

"Okay! Gosh!"

I turned the radio on a station that Rachel would like. She sang in the backseat, danced with her good arm and laughed at her mother and I as we joined her with our own silly moves.

"That's a pretty dress, Andi. You should wear dresses more often." Rachel commented.

"Should I? It's kind of hard to wear dresses when you ride horses for a living." I glanced over the seat at Rachel.

"You could ride side saddle, like women did in the old days!" The young girl pouted in thought.

"You know what? I'll do it if you do it!" I challenged.

"What? I'm not wearing a dress!" Rachel squawked.

"Oh my gosh!" her mother exclaimed. "Would you just go back to singing and be quiet? Sometimes you talk too much young lady!"

Cole rolled the car to a stop in front of Rachel's house. He pushed his door opened, then opened the back door for Rachel and helped her down.

"He really is a catch, Andi. You better hang onto him!" Rachel's mother whispered over the back of my seat.

"Yes, he is," I agreed, but something nagged in the back of my mind as I said it. "I'll try," I smiled over my shoulder.

"Thank you so much, Cole, Andi! You should both come over for dinner some time. We would love to have you."

"We'll do that... soon," I told Rachel's mom through the open car window as I waved.

Cole waited until they were in the house, then steered the car around the circle driveway and back toward the road. He stopped at the end of my driveway, turned to me, and stroked my hair. "Let's skip the awards thing, go back to your place. I think we should talk."

"What?" I wanted nothing more than to clear the air about the phone messages, but this award was important to Cole. "It's important for you! Why would you want to blow it off?" I don't know what was worse, him missing this award or me learning the truth. I wanted this love between us to be real. Though part of me still felt he was behind the messages, I knew my heart and it had falling in love.

"Andi, some things in life are much more important than professional awards. I'm worried about you… about what you know, what you remember, sometimes what you're talking about."

What I remember? My intuition led me down the road of distrust again and I could feel my heart cracking, my mind slipping, but I held on with all I had left. This was what I had wanted when I said yes to his date offer. I wanted to know the truth. But what about after the truth? Was my life at stake? If I couldn't win Cole over, did I care anymore?

"You're right. We need to clear the air, get some things out in the open." I nodded. It was time, wasn't it?

"I'll make us some lunch. We can change into something more comfortable. We'll talk." He pulled his lower lip between his teeth. "I have some very important things to tell you, Andi."

"I know you do." The color drained from my face as he turned away. My mind went blank. Then suddenly, I envisioned walking through my house and as I did, I sought weapons to protect myself. Mentally, I ticked off any items I could grab as I passed through each room. Whatever the outcome of this nightmare, I decided it was better to fight.

"Good." He nodded and pulled into my driveway.

He was an amazing man. It was too bad it had to end this way.

And he drove so well.

I couldn't let him go, but how could I keep him after the torment of texts?

8 months, 4 days and 3 hours ago… something happened. What happened?

A gentle rain fell softly outside the living room window. I moved along the row of windows to open them. I watched the drops as I curled my pajama clad legs under me and listened to the soft pinging on the metal roof of the porch.

Cole picked up the plate on the table before me. "Better?" he asked.

"Yes, much. Thank you for making lunch." A wisp of a smile lifted my lips then disappeared again.

"For you, beautiful, anything." He tilted my chin to look into my eyes. He nodded solemnly.

"What is it?" I frowned.

"That look… That dark place you've been in, I think it's gone. You're better, back to normal. We can talk now."

I searched his eyes deeply. God, he was amazing! I still didn't even know him, but he took such good care of me. He loved me. I could see the love in his soft eyes. I had to be better so he wouldn't go away. No more crazy tears, no more darkness. I shook my head and turned from him. Only happy tears from now on, right? At least until the truth comes out, which would be any second now. Part of me knew he was the one torturing me, but why would he? If the love I saw in his face was real, then why?

The rain beat harder against the metal roof. The horses would be in their stalls now. A rumble in the distance announced the severity of a coming storm. I loved storms. We should be in bed, not talking about reasons or excuses or whatever truths I thought I wanted, needed.

Was I ready to hear it?

Cole handed me a glass of wine. "This early?" I took it. Wine just made everything better sometimes.

"Why not? We're celebrating!" He sat next to me on the couch.

"Celebrating? What? Rachel?" I asked in shock.

"Sure, the return of Rachel, the precocious preteen! To Rachel!"

I clinked my glass against his, twirled the glass by its stem, taking in the aroma, then I brought the glass to my lips. I wasn't much of an afternoon drinker, but today with the rain, the past week, it just felt good. Twirl, twirl, the dim light in the house, the lightning outside, the soft red liquid swirling, tinting then clearing from the glass. I felt warm, comfortable, whole, healthy, loved.

"Andi, what did you see when you looked at my phone?" Cole focused on the red wine in his glass as he asked the question.

I stopped swirling, reached out and set the glass down on the coffee table. "Nothing. I didn't look at your phone. You took it with you, remember, when you left me?" I shook away the image of his phone in my hand.

"I didn't leave you, Andi. Would you get that out of your mind? I'm here. I only left for a little while. Then I came back. I'm still here. Don't say it that way. I'm here." Cole touched my shoulder, but his touch felt different somehow.

"That's what I meant." I nodded, turning away from him to watch the heavy drops falling outside, waterfalls running off the porch roof.

"Do you want to look at my phone now?" He freed his phone from his pocket.

A deep sadness filled me. I didn't want the truth. I didn't care why he was sending them. "No, not now. It couldn't have been you. Just hold me." I moved closer to him, snuggled up to his chest. His arm wrapped around me, so strong and safe and gentle.

"We need to talk, now. You'll understand if you just try. Try to listen. It will all be over soon." His warm breath against the crown of my head, his soft stroking of my hair, the beating of his strong heart comforted me. "Now that you're well, you'll understand."

"I was never sick," I said flatly into his chest. I had to be well. He would leave me like Matt did.

"I didn't mean that. I meant... we just need to talk. Tell me what's been bothering you and what you saw."

I pushed away from him, straightened, looked up at his strong face. He stroked my chin with his fingertip, cupped it in his hand, and kissed me— a tender, final kiss that reached into my heart and separated it further, a goodbye type of kiss.

I felt the sting of tears, but they weren't the same as the crazy tears. It had to be done, out in the open. "Okay, first, there was the accident," I began.

"Rachel's accident?"

"No, the other one...with the bicycle. It was before Rachel, before you, before Matt left me." A lone tear escaped the corner of my eye slowly working its way down my cheek.

"Matt, your fiancé?" Cole tilted his head to better view my downturned face.

"Yes," I nodded twice. It felt so good to talk about it. I wanted to keep talking.

"I was driving…" it was a long time ago, wasn't it? "…and the bicycle just came out of nowhere, right in front of me. I don't know who it was. I never had the nerve to find out. But today, at the hospital, I wanted to know, to find him or her. I was looking for the person I hit, but I didn't know who it was. I never found out who it was!" The tears flowed heavier to match the rhythm of the falls from the rooftop. The pent up guilt released the hard tangled knot in my stomach. I hadn't realized how much guilt consumed me until the knot released, disbursed, and exited my body in a flood of tears. "It was the guilt that made me crazy. That's why Matt left me. I lost it." Closing my eyes to stop the flood, I wiped at my wet cheeks with my fingers.

"Mhm," Cole nodded, his hand softly stroking my hair.

"See… I was sending Matt a text message. It was this crazy little thing we did at any time of the day. But that day, I was late for work. As I drove through the cold morning to the office, I thought of Matt and I had to text him."

Why was I driving to work? Matt always drove me to work.

"What kind of text? What did it say?" Cole prodded.

Could I tell Cole? Didn't he already know? I had come this far already. I needed to say it out loud. I'd felt better with each word. *Just say it,* my inner self urged. But this would be it. This would be the moment of truth. Everything would be on the table.

Then what?

Just say it, I told myself. Yes, I could say it. My damp eyes met his as I said "BTW, I love you." I watched him closely. The muscles in his face tensed, then quickly relaxed.

Keep going.

"As I typed it in, this tire appeared in my peripheral vision. I stomped the brake, but it was too late. I never sent the message. The last thing I saw was my phone on the floor beneath the steering wheel, the unsent message glaring at me. Guilt and shock consumed me, and I blacked out." My mind was clear now. My stomach relaxed. It was out now— my truth. Soon, I would know his truth.

"What happened when you woke up?" he asked, stroking a stray tear from my cheek.

"I don't know. That part is fuzzy. But, later, I went crazy from the guilt, and Matt left me. I don't blame him I pushed him away really. It was our text message that hurt that cyclist. It was our text message that came between our love, tore us apart. Matt finally gave up on me, hated me, I think. He fell in love with someone else.

I don't blame him," I repeated that one phrase, even though I had blamed him. Did I still?

My phone buzzed, lit up, went silent on the table by my wine glass.

Lightning lit the sky outside the window; a loud boom followed closely behind intensifying the storm inside and out.

The rain pounded the world beyond the window. We so needed that rain. It was a good thing for the seed planted in the back pasture. I smiled about the rain.

"Are you going to check that?" Cole indicated the phone with his eyes. I glanced toward him, then down at my phone on the table as a second buzz sounded.

"Hm? Oh, no. I know what it is. I don't need to look at it anymore." I picked up my wine glass, sipped, and set it down again.

"You're smiling," Cole noted.

"Yes. Rain is amazing, isn't it? It refreshes the world. Lightning cleans the air. Thunder makes a beautiful sound," I whispered.

"Storms are nice. I agree," Cole nodded.

"The best thing about storms is when they're over, everything is fresh and clean and begins anew with the sun." I added.

"Absolutely!" He took a strand of my hair between thumb and forefinger softly pulling the strand between them. "Aren't you even curious about the text message? I think you should look."

I ignored his request.

"What's on your phone, Andi? Who's texting you?" His gaze followed his fingers down the length of the strand as he nudged me gently back to the phone.

"I don't know who it is. I don't care. Somebody's trying to make me feel guilty, make me crazy, again. I just don't care anymore. I don't need to see it anymore. Drama!" I huffed.

"Can I look at your phone?" Cole asked.

"Sure. Help yourself!" My hand waved him toward another rattle of my phone.

"Would you like to look at mine, now? I mean, that's the only reason you accepted my date, right?" Cole asked as he picked up my phone.

What? "No, I'm over it, over that. I don't need to look. It's not you. It can't be you. You wouldn't do that to me." I stared out at the rain, a numbness filling my insides.

"What's not me, Andi? I wouldn't do what?" He asked as my phone lit his features.

"Send the text messages… torturing me with guilt… It's not you." I shook my head, sent a nervous smile his way.

Lightning, thunder, pitter patter of raindrops, now I felt it all. It felt good, refreshing. A brief curiosity flashed in my mind of whether death would feel this way.

And then, what I had known deep down would give me the answer. For as quickly as the calm came, it all went away with his next question, "How do you know it's not me?"

Turning back from the window, I caught a glimmer in his eyes, a glimmer of who he was when we met. The message from my phone reflected there, and when he looked up, I could see it clearly, "BTW, I love you."

I frowned.

His phone pinged next to him. He picked it up in

his free hand.

Holding my phone in one hand, he opened his in the other, looking at the text message. He turned both phones toward me and I saw the same, short message… one sent, one read. A gleam filled his eyes; the two phones returning the sting of tears, of panic.

It was the truth I didn't want to know! It had been him all along. Why?

"No!" I screamed pounding wildly on his arms and knocking both phones from his grasp! I pushed up and ran into the bedroom, ran away from him as the phones clattered to the floor. I slammed the door, locked it, leaned against it and cried madly. "No! No! No!"

His fists beat on the door, the rhythm matching the thunder outside the window. "Andi, stop! Let me in! You don't understand! You have to try to understand! Open the door!" I searched for something in my room, an object of protection, all the items I visualized before we entered my driveway seemed to have disappeared now. I needed something to defend myself should he break down the door.

He threw his body into the door, twisting the door jam, ripped the drywall and flung open the door.

"Don't come near me!" I screamed. "Leave me alone! Ever since the first day, I've known it was you! Why? Why would you do this to me? Why would you make me fall in love with you so you could rip it away like a nasty, old bandage?" I backed into my dresser, my hands searching feebly for something on top of it, anything!

"No! Andi, you're wrong!" He was coming toward me, his hands outstretched before him, moving closer to my throat.

Nothing! Nothing on my dresser but trinkets! I turned, swiped both hands over my dresser clearing the top just before his arms slipped around my waist, tightened, and lifted me off the floor.

My knees bent as I cried in anger, feet kicking, striking without aim.

He threw me on the bed pinning both my wrists beneath me with one hand and pressed his body onto mine,. With his free hand, he turned my face toward him, making me look into his distraught eyes. I wanted to bite him! I screamed, but I realized it was useless. Nobody could hear me over the storm.

"Stop!" he ordered calmly. "Just stop!" His now calm eyes affected my own as he frowned down at me. "God, you have beautiful eyes," he stroked my hair. I closed my eyes. I didn't want to look at him. "Please don't, Andi. Please open your eyes. Don't go there, back to the dark. I love you." His voice cracked with fear.

He was afraid?

Of me?

I opened my eyes.

Cole was still there. Not some crazed monster. Cole.

He hadn't left me.

He kissed me, soft at first, then harder, passionately until he found the love he knew, the love I needed, until he found the love that would keep me there with him, keep my eyes open, keep me loving him. He shifted to free my arms and my hands desperately sought his hair, the phones forgotten in the living room.

Again, I slept on his damp shoulder, the rain falling

softly on the metal roof. The storm had passed, leaving behind a sweet, calming rain.

It would be good for growth of the winter grasses.

I slept hard and long… hours passed as I dreamed of Cole's love, his touch, the pleasure and wonder of our life together.

The rain clouds moved away into the distance. I had forgotten the numbers. I didn't know why those silly numbers kept popping into my mind, the numbers above the haunting text messages… 84-384.

The messages… we would talk about those tomorrow, wouldn't we?

Cole's fingers stroked my hair, bringing me around to the sunlight filtering through the blinds. He was still next to me, his shoulder still beneath my head.

"You slept well." He placed a gentle kiss on the top of my head.

"Yes, I did. I think it was the storm." Tilting my head back, a contented smile filled my eyes.

"Which one?" he joked, recalling my rage.

"Oh, gosh! I'd forgotten. What came over me?" I sat up, the bedroom door half off and half on the twisted frame.

"You needed to get it out. I'll fix that door later today." He pulled me back to his chest.

"Yes, and now it is out, all of it. It was you, but you do love me, loved me even through my craziness."

"Andi, you were never crazy. Stop saying that." His chin rubbed my head as he shook disagreed.

"The sun's out." I felt chipper.

"Yes… Yes it is." He slipped his shoulder from beneath my head and rolled to his side to look at me.

"Tell me you love me."

"Are you ordering me again? First you order me to go on a date with you, now you order me to love you?" My brows raised.

Passion filled his face, the eyes that stared deep into mine, "Tell me you love me."

"Ask nicely," I rolled my eyes playfully away. The touch of his fingers on my chin turned me back to him.

"Tell me you love me."

How could I not? "I love you."

"Tell me you'll always love me, no matter what."

No matter what? Was there more I didn't know?

"You just like to control me!" I tried to lighten the mood.

"Tell me you'll always love me," he repeated.

"I'll always love you," I reassured him.

"No matter what?" He asked.

"No matter what," I repeated his words.

His mouth covered mine again.

I was alive.

Filled with passion, desire, strength, and love. Nothing else mattered. I didn't care what the "no matter what" meant.

The sun filtered through the blinds in the window waking me to start my day anew… again. Somehow, this morning felt different, in a good way. I'd slept so hard. How long had I been asleep this time?

I wanted to force my eyes open, but at the same time, the long rest felt so wonderful, peaceful, safe. I could stay this way forever.

"Andi! Andi!"

Someone called my name. A shadow passed between the window and my straining eyes, allowing me to open my lids slowly to the bright light.

It hurt to open my eyes. Did the wine cause this headache?

It wasn't Cole's voice calling me. Whose voice, then?

"Andi! She's waking up! Andi!" A young female voice exclaimed, her excitement filling the room.

Rachel?

Oh, no, the horses! How could I keep forgetting my horses? What was with me these days?

"What?" I tried to speak, but my throat hurt. No sound escaped my lips. There was a hand, a hand stroking back my hair.

"Back up, honey! Let the doctors and nurses do their thing." A strong voice, Cole's voice, the voice in my ear, in my thoughts, all this time, all this time after Matt left.

Buzz.

Buzz.

Buzz.

Buzz.

"Andi?" A whispered breath touched my lips. "Andi? Are you with me? Can you hear me?"

My eyes searched the flecks of blue, green, gray in his tender eyes, searched his strong, handsome face, his whiskered chin. My gaze wandered beyond his face, to the window, the walls, the whoosh of the opening door. Who came into my room behind him?

"Do you know me, Andi? Do you?" His deep voice whispered from the lips hovering above me. I smiled at the question.

"Of course, silly." I blinked. My hoarse voice whispered again, "Of course, I do." What was wrong with my voice? It hurt to talk. My mouth was so dry. "I love you," I croaked.

"*What* did she say?" Rachel asked.

My eyes rolled toward her and I smiled.

"Where am I?" I frowned at Rachel.

Rachel put her hand on my head, "In the hospital.

Don't you remember?"

"No."

Cole moved out of the way. A nurse and doctor moved in.

The doctor lifted first one eyelid, then the other; he shined a light in each of my eyes. The light hurt my eyes. Laying a cold object on my chest, the doctor listened. What was happening?

Buzz.

Buzz.

Buzz.

Buzz.

Beep.

Beep.

I frowned. Rachel dropped some small ice chips in my mouth. They melted and I swallowed.

Buzz.

Buzz.

Buzz.

"Will somebody please turn off my cellphone?" I grumbled hoarsely.

"Cell phone?" Rachel looked up at Cole. "Dad, did you tell her?"

Cole nodded.

Wait! Dad?

"It's a miracle. Everything sounds perfect. It's like she was never in a coma."

Coma?

"Limit your time. Don't make her talk too much. And you keep the excitement down, young lady!" The doctor shook a chubby finger at Rachel.

"When can she go home, Doc?" Cole stood near as

the doctor left.

"We'll have to play it by ear. This is a remarkable recovery, though. Guess her body just needed that much time to heal."

Recovery? Did I fall off of Thunder? I thought.

"But, if she keeps improving, we'll get some PT in and maybe within the week, providing she comes back for therapy." The doctor nodded at Cole and left the room.

Buzz.

Buzz.

Cole turned his broad shoulders toward me as the nurse turned the volume down on a few machines.

Silence.

The nurse handed Rachel a pitcher and instructed her to get some water. Rachel vanished and the nurse touched Cole's back, then followed the young girl out the door. Cole's wide shoulders rose, fell, shook.

Breathe.

Breathe.

In and out, I silently instructed him as he stood there quivering.

The words floated through my mind, somehow reaching him. He inhaled deeply, let it out, and took another breath.

Finally he turned toward me, moved to the edge of my bed and sat, picking up my hand.

My hand looked so frail, so pale, next to his. It shouldn't be like that. I spent most days outside, with the horses, on the tractor. I frowned at my hand in his.

"Andi? Are you okay?" A look of concern crossed his face.

"My hand…" I stared at my hand in his.

He looked down at the back of my hand, raised it to his lips, and kissed it tenderly.

Rachel returned with the water, poured a glass, and I sipped greedily. My throat was so dry.

"Was it Thunder?" I looked at Rachel.

"Well, it was thundering, but the storm's gone now," Rachel answered.

I laughed at her confusion.

"No, the horse, silly? Thunder?"

"Huh?" Rachel looked at Cole. "Is she talking about *the* Thunder?" Rachel's eyes widened.

"Yeah. Yeah, I think she is," Cole answered.

"You told her about *Thunder?*" Rachel seemed afraid.

"Mhm. And Winks, and the foals and anything I could tell her to keep her here listening."

Rachel's face grew serious as she stared at the man across from her, too serious for such a young girl.

"Did you tell her the truth, Dad?" The look Rachel sent him struck a nerve in me. *The truth?*

"I was getting to it, then you came back in, and she woke up…"

"Are you hungry, Andi? Would you like some jello? Or ice cream? I would!" Rachel held her hand out to Cole, who obediently laid a ten dollar bill in her hand.

"Chocolate, please," I croaked, trying to lift myself to a sitting position. My muscles trembled with the effort. A wave of dizziness forced me back down.

"You got it! BRB!" The young girl's curly, blond, ponytail swung behind her as she flung open the door and disappeared down the hall.

"Let me help you," Cole propped another pillow behind me and lifted gently so I was sitting up. Then he took the water cup in hand, poured some from the pitcher, and offered me a sip. It felt so good going down that I wanted to drink it all in one gulp.

"Little sips," Cole reminded.

"BRB?" I searched Cole's face.

"Be right back," he shrugged. "Kid and texts, right?" He joked, but his face was far from tickled.

"Wait, did she call you Dad?" I bit my lower lip, bringing pain to it from the dryness.

"Yes, she did. That's right," Cole smiled sadly at me.

"Cole, why am I in the hospital? The last thing I remember is you and me in my bedroom, on the ranch, the storm outside, the…" I felt my face flush.

"Hmpf, interesting. Tell me more," he smiled playfully, his brows rising in facetiousness.

"No, no. Answer me, first. Why am I here?" My neck seemed so weak, so heavy. I let my head fall back onto the top of the pillows.

"Let me raise you up some more." He pulled one pillow up higher and raised the head of the bed with the crank so I could lay back and still see him.

He returned to his seat, picked up my hand, and kissed it again.

"Well?" I searched his face, the joy slipping away when I noticed the glaze of unshed tears in his eyes.

"Andi… you were hit by a car. Don't you remember?" *Hit by a car? Me? While riding Thunder?*

I closed my eyes to pull the memory free, but nothing came except the tire.

"Open your eyes, please. Don't ever close your eyes, again. Never for longer than a good night's sleep. Keep them open, Andi, please." The hurt in his eyes, when I did open them, touched my heart and shredded it to pieces.

He lifted a strand of golden brown hair, wound the waves around his fingers, and let it go.

"Okay, they're open. The tire, I just closed them to remember, but all I could see was the tire..." the tire from the top as if... "I didn't go to the hospital, then. The ambulance came and picked up the person on the bicycle. Is that person okay?" Suddenly, it became very important that I learn the fate of the person on the bicycle. "Oh my gosh! What happened to the person I hit?"

"She's in the hospital. Andi..." Cole paused and thought carefully about his next words, "It was your bicycle tire. You were riding the bicycle." He said each word slowly as if I needed to hear them that way to accept the truth. A tear escaped his eye, slipped down the groove of his nose, dripped over his lips and splashed on our joined hands.

It was warm and wet, like the rain showers, leaving behind a cooled, damp streak that settled where our palms connected.

"My tire? No, no I hit someone on a bicycle... with my car. I told you that before. I was sending a text message to Matt, and I..." I frowned, pausing mid sentence. *That is what happened, wasn't it?*

"No, Andi, I was sending the text message, to..." The door squeaked open, and Rachel entered carrying small containers of ice cream in one hand and dollar bills in the other. "... Rachel." He said as he glanced up at the girl who claimed to be his daughter. His words sounded familiar. I struggled to remember, put the pieces together. I scanned Rachel's face, her hands full of ice cream and money. Cole held his hand out to Rachel, "Change?"

"Aw, dad!" She handed it over.

"Wait! Your cast?" I looked at Rachel's left arm.

"Cast?" A goofy confused look passed over her, then she grinned, "You told her *that*?" She squeaked at Cole. "He told you about my broken arm? About Trooper? Oh, jeez, Dad!" She shook her head and pulled the tab up on the ice cream.

"Need help with this?" She asked me sweetly. I lifted my hand with the IV tube taped to it. The heavy feeling caused my arm to tremble.

"No, I think I can do it." The ice cream was soft enough that the little plastic spoon slipped right into it.

The icy container sat cupped in my hand, I took the plastic spoon with the other and lifted it to my mouth, but hit my chin. They laughed; so did I. "Well, that never happens!" I rolled my eyes as Rachel handed me a napkin.

"Well, it is the first time you've fed yourself in a long time. Let me help you," Cole took the container and spoon from me, my hands falling to my sides.

"I broke my arm two years ago," Rachel filled in.

"*Two years?*" My head shook, back and forth. No, that couldn't be right! The words Cole spoke before Rachel came back returned to me. "So, wait! It was my tire and your phone. You were texting Rachel?" I said between bites. I took three, turning away from the fourth, my stomach churning. He nodded, finishing the tiny carton of chocolate ice cream.

"Jeez, Dad, could you be any slower at telling her? I mean, you told her everything else!" Rachel shrugged.

"Rachel, it's going to take time. Stop hounding." He cast a firm look at her.

"Telling me? Telling me… what?"

"Well, I'm going to the waiting room to watch TV. If I fall asleep out there, wake me up when it's time to go, okay? *Gosh*!" Rachel left the room, again.

Cole set the carton aside. He took both my hands in his. He smiled calmly, playfully. "Tell me that you will always love me, no matter what."

How could I not? I already did, hadn't I?

"This again? Really? You're so bossy!" I shook my head, but I looked up at him and smiled. He was confused.

Something wasn't right.

"Again?" he asked.

The pieces were starting to fall into place. Rachel's arm, my tire, his text message. My eyes widened as I peered up at him.

"Matt!"

"He left not long after they told him you were in a coma. He seemed relieved actually. Something wasn't right about his response to that, Andi, so I did some digging afterward. We can talk about that later, though. It doesn't matter, now. I stayed here with you. There hasn't been a day that I haven't been here to sit near you, to talk to you, keep you going, keep you alive and give you a reason to return to the world."

"You?" I was starting to understand. But this

couldn't be right! I shook my head, refused to believe his words. "What do you mean Matt left? Matt left me in the hospital? That can't be!" Suddenly, I was nauseous.

Cole nodded sadly. "He did. There's more, Andi. You were pretty beat up when you got here. Even the doctor said it wasn't likely that that minor car accident caused most of your injuries. About two weeks after you came here, Matt came back. I'd had to run a bank errand, and thought I would stop in to visit you. When I got to the window, I saw him standing over you…" Cole paused when he saw the look of confusion darken my face. "It's not important! What's important is you're back to normal, well, almost."

"No, no I want to know about Matt. Why was I beat up? What happened? Are you telling me…"

"Andi, it's really not important. You've been through so much. Please, we'll talk about that another time, when you're out of here and better." Cole touched my cheek lightly.

"No, tell me now." I stated calmly. Somewhere in my memories, a sense of panic, danger, filled me and I needed to know why.

Alright." Cole relented. "Matt's hands were at your neck. I asked him what he thought he was doing. It startled him and he ran off. I told the nurse about it. He never came back. If he did, they didn't let him see you."

"Are you saying, Matt tried to…" I couldn't believe what he was telling me. Matt was the love of my life! He wouldn't do that! Cole had to be lying. He was trying to minimize his part in the accident!

"You were driving the car that hit me? You hit me!" My voice rose, my breaths came rapidly, shallowly.

The memory of the accident returned and tears started flowing. I tried to pull my hands from his. "You hit me!" I couldn't catch my breath. My chest hurt. My monitor beeped frantically.

"You… were… texting Rachel…" I gulped air.

"Your truck came at me…" It was so hard to breathe!

"*You* were late for work! Not me!" I gasped for air.

"I didn't look either way. You always look both ways!" I remembered his careful driving in my dreams.

"I was angry, no not angry, scared. I was… fleeing from… oh my god, Matt… Matt was so angry? I took off on my bicycle to get… I didn't look! I didn't look!" The hot, angry, crazy tears streaked my cheeks, dropped onto my hospital gown, dampened my chest. The machines beeped and buzzed madly next to me.

"How long? How long have I been here?" I heaved out the words, feeling as though an elephant pressed into my chest. Cole drew a tissue from the box on the night stand. He dabbed my cheeks, though he should have dried his own.

He offered me a sip of water from my glass; my throat hurt. "How long ago was the accident?" I asked again, pushing away his hand and the cup of water so forcefully that it hit the floor. Cole's hands dropped to his lap. His gaze turned to his hands. His shoulders shook heavily, then they stopped. His reddened eyes found mine.

"Eight months, four days and three hours. Today was the day. Today, they were going to let you go. They had removed the ventilator tubing and… but I knew… I wouldn't let them do anything else because you breathed on your own. Even though they told me it wouldn't last, I knew. I knew if I kept talking to you that you would come back... you would come back *to me*." His fingers reached for my cheek. The sincerity in his eyes touched my heart, pulled at it, drew it to him, but I stopped it. He had put me here, in this hospital, in this condition! His neglectful actions had cost me everything! My life, my job, my home, I wasn't thinking clearly.

Those numbers shuffled through my mind, those horrifying numbers, 8... 4... 3.

I couldn't believe what was happening, how my dreams had misled me!

Though Cole tried hard to comfort me, to apologize, to bring me around to him, I couldn't deal with it. My breathing grew more stressed and I nearly choked in anger with his every action. The nurse rushed into the room as the machines violently sounded and she asked Cole to leave.

As the door slid closed behind him, Cole's head slumped toward his chest and he leaned his back into the clear glass. His shoulders trembled.

The nurse adjusted my oxygen, checked my vitals, lowered the bed, and told me she would get me some medicine to help me rest, but how could I? Finally, after the medicine kicked in, I slept. As the nurse's blurring figure left the room, she touched Cole's arm and said something I couldn't hear, something about hope, something about anxiety and natural. Cole disappeared down the hallway in the direction Rachel had gone earlier.

Closing my eyes, I replayed the conversation the three of us shared. It left me with a familiar feeling… a family feeling. How could I feel that way about somebody who hit me with his car? Before long, I slept again. I don't know how long, but every hour the nurses returned to check my vitals. The cafeteria staff brought food. The doctor came back every day. The physical therapist came three times a day.

Within a week, I felt strong enough to stand, take walks down the hallway.

At the end of the first week, Rachel returned. It was a Friday afternoon. She'd taken a different bus from the school, then another into town.

"Hi, Andi." She smiled tentatively as she entered. She was so sweet. I couldn't blame her for the accident.

"Hey!" I tried to smile. "Come on in. Sit down." I sat opposite her in the recliner and crossed my legs. The old sweats I wore were loose from loss of muscle tone, but they still fit. They'd been left in the closet of the room. I guessed Matt must have brought them in hopes I would wake up.

"I saw you coming back from your walk. I was in the waiting room. Here!" She stuck out her hand to give me a small floral bouquet in a vase.

"Thanks." I didn't mean for it to be, but the tension was thick.

"You look like you're doing good!" She offered, biting her lower lip.

"Yeah… uhm… the doctor says I'm getting stronger every day. I should be ready to go home soon… wherever that is." The thought confused me momentarily. Had Matt sold our home?

"I miss you," Rachel looked down at her hands in her lap, then back up at me.

"Miss me?" That was an odd thing to tell me.

"Well, I mean, we've been spending so much time here. Almost every day after school… most weekends. It just felt weird, not being here all week. I didn't have anyone to talk to." She shrugged.

"Oh, yeah. I bet I was a pretty good listener." I couldn't help but smile at her.

Rachel's features relaxed.

"Look, Rachel, this is… I don't know, it's just so weird to me. I knew you as my neighbor, while I was in the coma. To wake up and learn that nothing I thought was true was actually the truth— it's just, it's hard to process." I took in a deep breath, let it out in an overwhelmed sigh.

"I can leave if you want… if you'd be more

comfortable." The girl stood.

"No… Uhm… I don't know, Rachel. I've been really lonely, even with all the medical attention." I looked at my hands folded in my lap.

"Or, I can stay and answer your questions… the ones I can answer, anyway." She shrugged.

I thought about her offer. There were some things I would have to know before I left, I guess. For one, where was I supposed to go?

"Cole… Uhm, your dad said my fiancé left me. Do you know anything about that?" My nose wrinkled curiously.

Rachel's face flushed and her nostrils flared. Her anger made her look away from me. When she turned back to me, she'd calmed a little. "Yes, actually, I know everything about it. I was here the day he and Dad got into it and Matt ran out. But there was one time I came in before that and overheard Matt talking to you. Dad and I had been coming up here to relieve Matt for a few weeks. Then one day, I came alone and heard Matt telling you he was sorry for what he did. He couldn't risk you waking up and causing problems for him, though. And then he just lost it! He told him he didn't know what to do about you, after your big fight, after you ran off. He was sorry he lost his temper with you, struck you, but he didn't know what would happen now. He said he couldn't risk starting over then having you wake up and remember everything. He said something about being lucky that man came along and ran into your bike. Then the nurse came over to me because she noticed I hadn't gone inside your room, and she made him leave. She called security and everything." Rachel paused. "I didn't tell Dad about that day."

What? Things had been so wonderful with Matt and me before the accident! Matt and I were so in love… weren't we? I frowned, trying to remember.

"Matt yelled at the hospital staff that it was none of their business. He said, you were never going to come back and he didn't have time to wait around for you anyway. He told me Dad and I were welcome to keep coming up here as often as we liked and wait, but we shouldn't hold our breath! They took him away and he never came back." She paused again.

"What?" Stunned, my jaw fell open as I stared at her.

"Yeah, it was actually pretty bad. I was scared, for me and for you." She wrinkled her nose in fear. "That Matt, he was talking like you were dead already. I knew you weren't. Don't ask me how. Dad and I just knew." She smiled at me, warm and reassuring.

I glanced away. "What about our house? Do you know anything about it?"

Her cheeks filled with air, then she let it out through pursed lips. "Yeah. We've been by a few times, on the way home. It's been sold. It looks like a family lives there now, some kid stuff in the front yard. I'm sorry, Andi!" She could see the hurt in my face. She took my hand in hers. "Maybe I shouldn't have told you."

"No. I needed to know. I have to make plans for when I get out of here, right?" I nodded.

"Wh… what are your plans, if you don't mind me asking? I mean, do you have some family to stay with?" She squeezed my hand gently.

"Hmm… no, actually. My family is gone. I suppose

Matt didn't leave our bank account open, either. I don't know what I'm going to do." I shook my head.

"Uhm… can I help you with anything? Get you anything?" Rachel offered.

"Actually, if you can find out if I had a bank card, or any money in an account somewhere, that would be great. I don't know what I'm going to do when they release me." Suddenly, I felt more alone than ever.

"Sure. I can do that. Don't worry, Andi. Just keep getting better." She squeezed my hand again. "I have to go so I'm home before Dad gets there. Ever since the accident, he's been… protective."

"Of course! Go! Just let me know what you find out. You can call. You don't have to come back up here and risk getting in trouble." I pulled my hand free of hers and shooed her to the door.

She turned before the door opened and bit her lower lip as she prepared to tell me something I knew she probably shouldn't. "Dad— well, he feels really bad, Andi. He hasn't been the same since he told you. It's like… he's lost or something." Then she turned after exiting the open door. My eyes followed her till I could no longer see her. It wasn't until after she'd been gone for sometime that I picked up the flowers she'd brought. I inhaled their scent, bringing a memory of my flower beds in front of my home. Slowly, my past returned to me. I made a mental not to ask the nurse if they'd taken and pictures of me when I arrived at the hospital.

When I set the flowers back on the stand, the card fell free. I bent to pick it up, stabilizing myself with one hand on the bed rail.

I*n case you need anything* was inscribed on the outside of the small envelope. I removed the small card from within. It was a business card. *Blue Stone Ranch* written in a blue font with the address and phone number in black below it. *Quarter Horse Breeding and Sales* was written at the bottom.

I turned the card over and started to replace it when I noticed the handwriting in ink on the backside.

Anything! Cole and Rachel Blake.

"So, that's his last name," I whispered to myself, a faint smile crossing my lips.

The volunteer came in just as I replaced the card. A clothing bag hung over one arm, a box of shoes in the other. She smiled, "I'll just put these in the closet for when you go home." She hung up the bag and placed the shoes in the bottom. "There's an extra lounge set in the bag if you want us to wash those sweats anytime soon. I'll be happy to send them out for cleaning for you."

"Oh," I looked down at the brightly colored outfit my body was swimming in now. "Thanks. Where did those come from?"

"I don't really know. The front desk sent me up with them. There's more, so when you get ready to leave, they're yours! I'll bring them up later. Don't over tax yourself. PT takes a lot out of you. Get some rest. Oh, and I put some books in your nightstand while you were at PT. Also, a cellphone? It was left at the front desk for you, as well." She smiled as she left the room. I went to the closet to explore my clothes options. Everything inside would be baggy for now, but I found a silk lounge set to put on. I rolled the sweats into a laundry bag and put them in the floor of the closet. It felt good to wear something beside a hospital gown or sweats.

I laid back on the bed, my energy waning. Rolling to my side, I opened the night stand drawer and selected a book. The cellphone was new and a blue sticky note curled upward on the screen. Memories from my dreams filled me with apprehension as I withdrew the phone and charger, I read the sticky note:

My number's in the phone. Anything!
Cole

Tears blurred the phone screen.

Suddenly I was angry! He left me a cellphone? It was him and his cellphone that cost me Matt, my home, my life! What was he thinking?

I chucked the phone and charger back into the drawer and rolled to my side, crying myself to a restless sleep filled with leftover comatose dreams.

When I woke up, the dinner tray was sitting on my bed table. I had never been much for watching TV, but I reached for the remote and pushed the ON button. I needed distraction.

Pulling the roller table to a chair, I removed the rounded plate cover. The scented steam of potatoes and meatloaf wafted upward. The salad looked amazing! My stomach growled in response. I was famished! Scanning the channels, I found a game show to watch. When the cafeteria lady came back to retrieve the tray, she was shocked. "You must like meat loaf!"

"Actually, I barely tasted it. And I'm still hungry. Is there a way I can get anything else?" I begged.

"Sure! Let me see what I can find for you."

A volunteer returned a half hour later with another dinner tray. This time I took my time, tasting it all. Even the roll was delicious. It was as if I'd awakened for the first time in my life and discovered food. I was so full I moved to the bed and fell into a deep sleep, the TV the only light emanating inside the dark room.

The next morning, the doctor told me I needed one more week of in hospital physical therapy before I was released. Then I would need to return for therapy three times a week for the next eight weeks. He was glad to see I had eaten and wanted to see me put on a little more weight. He ordered me to eat whenever I felt the need and left word with the nurses station to make sure I did. Physical therapy was taking as much out of me as I was putting into my body. Then the doctor produced the folder I inquired about. "These are copies of the pictures that we took the day you arrived. According to the police report and the witness testimony, the truck wasn't going fast enough to do anything more than knock your bicycle over. These pictures indicate there was more to the story of how you arrived here than you know. If you begin feeling anxious, don't look at them. Promise?" When I acquiesced, he sent a look of caution my way and left me alone to peruse the day I arrived here.

I didn't even recognize myself.

Three times a day, I went for PT. A psychiatrist met me in my room once a day to help me, "sort things out".

My strength returned gradually. Between therapy sessions and medical visits, I ate as much as I could take in. Reading the books in the drawer helped pass time between sessions and tests… and keep me from thinking about the day I arrived. I was free to walk down the hall anytime I wanted now because my muscles were stabilizing and the tremors were gone. Rachel stopped by a couple of times on her way home just to visit, so we walked out to the hospital garden to talk. The floral blooms' aroma instantly calmed me. Lavender, honeysuckle, and other scents I couldn't recall. My eyes settled on a unique blue rose growing opposite where Rachel and I sat. I couldn't take my eyes from it as she talked.

Rachel was a sweet girl. She'd learned from her research that I did in fact have a bank account with a bank card. She wouldn't tell me how she discovered the information except to say a friend helped her. She had told the bank she was my niece and that I was in the hospital in need of cash for when I was released. The card would be delivered to the hospital by the end of the week.

Though I hadn't asked, Rachel told me Cole set up a hotel room for me as soon as he learned I would be released the following week. I couldn't get over how much I felt that I loved this girl, though I barely knew her. It was as if I had known her forever. Not knowing what would come of my life after release, I hoped I wouldn't have to let our newfound friendship fade.

It seemed odd to me how I could picture in my comatose state exactly how Rachel looked in real life. And Cole… well, he was exactly as I pictured, too.

At least once a day, I took the cellphone from the drawer, turned it on to call him, then shut it down again. I didn't need— or want— anything. My anger toward Cole had not diminished.

After a few phone calls from my hospital phone, I learned my old position at work, of course, had been filled. I didn't know the new editor, either, so nothing was accomplished. So much had changed at the magazine. What was I going to do when I got out of the hospital?

Physical therapy helped work out my thoughts and anger, though the therapists stopped me numerous times during each session because I was pushing myself too hard. I couldn't help it. I just wanted my old life back, but it wasn't looking promising.

Flowers arrived every day; a variety of bouquets now filled my hospital room… all from Cole. One day I returned from testing to find a bouquet of a dozen two tone white and pink roses centered perfectly among baby's breath and greenery, the same bouquet Matt always bought for me. Matt?

I hurried to the tall vase, pulled the envelope free, and then slipped the card out, a rush of mixed emotions topped with terror flooded me. Since I'd reviewed the pictures numerous times, I remembered what had happened that day. Turning over the Heal Quickly note, I read the back. It was definitely Matt's handwriting! My heart flip flopped and I dropped the card in fear.

* * *

Happy to hear you are awake and on the mend. I would like to see you, but I understand if you don't want to see me. Here's my new cell number. If you need anything…
Matt

How did he know? I'd learned from a secretary at the magazine that Matt had married someone else a few months after I was hospitalized… another girl from the magazine that he'd met at an office party. I wondered about her safety, about their life together.

Yes, Matt, I need something. I need you, I thought as I picked up the card, a new boldness filling my chest. "I need you to leave me alone!" I flung the card into the trash and started for the vase when the realization hit me. I was truly on my own, now. Monday I would be released and I would be alone. I felt lost. I hadn't been on my own in my entire life. Falling back onto the bed, I closed my eyes and relived the life I'd had in my dreams… the life I'd had with Cole and Rachel. But it wasn't my life; it was their life.

I was not the type to give up, though. No matter that I was starting over. I could do it, and I knew I could. When my bank card arrived, I called customer service to find out how much I had in my account. Turns out there was an incredible amount of money in my account. I don't even know how it built up to that during my hospital stay. Matt took care of the finances when we were together; I never even asked about money. Maybe, out of guilt, he'd left an account for my medical expenses. Briefly I thought to call him and ask, but it still stung that he became so infuriated that day that he beat me. Then, that he would leave me while I was in the hospital. I understood that he hoped I wouldn't recover, likely so I wouldn't press criminal charges on him, but the fact that he gave up on our love—a love I felt would last forever—hurt more than a beating ever could. Try as I might, I remembered the angry words we spoke that day, but I couldn't remember him striking me. It didn't matter; I never wanted to see or talk to him again. Still, I couldn't remember if I provoked it or not. Fortunately, I would never have to see him again, unlike so many relationships that involved children... unless I pressed charges, which I had been considering with the help of my psychiatrist. Closure, the psychiatrist called it. I called it justice. I always thought one day we would start a family

Children... hmm, my planning with Matt now seemed a distant dream.

Rachel...

If there was a daughter in my future, she would be just like Rachel.

I sat up and used the cellphone Cole left me to create my online banking profile so I could start making plans. After scheduling a car to pick me up, I called the hotel to tell them I would be there Monday. Then I searched the internet on my borrowed phone for jobs that fit my skills. The money in my account was substantial enough to last me a while, long past physical therapy, but I needed something to do.

Five more days and I would be leaving, starting my life over again, but something was missing and it left a giant, empty hole right in the center of my chest.

Sunday night one of my doctors visited my room to prepare me for discharge, "You are almost as fit as you were eight months ago when you came to us—minus the physical damage." He flipped through my chart, watched the nurse as she checked my vitals, and shook his head. "It's a real life miracle. I'm glad you woke up when you did," he smiled, signed another paper, then handed the chart to the nurse. "So, what are you off to conquer now that you've had eight months of rest?"

I shrugged in response, "I don't know."

"Well, maybe that nice looking guy who stayed by your side all these months will be able to help you out with that! That's one spunky little girl he has on his hands. Pretty sure he could handle another feisty one, though. Take care. I don't want to see you back in here, now!" He patted my arm and left the room.

The nurse cocked her head and smiled at me.

"The doctors kind of grew to like that man of yours. Where's he been? I've seen his daughter hanging around. Is he picking you up tomorrow?"

She meant Cole. What made her think he was "my guy"? Did she not know why he was up here all the time? It was obvious to me he felt guilty about the accident. Why had they not seen that? Or, did they not know he was the one who hit my bicycle?

"No. I have a car coming to pick me up." The words came out colder than I intended.

"Oh, I'm sorry, I didn't mean to pry. Well, we're almost ready to get you out of here first thing in the morning. Just need PT to sign off and nobody's down there until tomorrow morning. Let me know if you need anything." The nurse never skipped a beat while performing her tasks. I was glad to see that my cold demeanor had not stirred her or changed her mood. Of course, medical staff had to be used to various types of natures and certainly trained to not take the moods of patients personally.

Dinner arrived on the tray, and the staff member joked about it being the best in the house for my last meal. I smiled and thanked her, but after she left, I wasn't very hungry. The cell phone in one hand and my fork picking through the contents on the plate with the other, I touched the contacts button and found Cole's number.

His picture, I was certain Rachel had taken and uploaded to the placeholder, stared back at me.

Closing my eyes, I relived our dance in the house, our trip to the bar, our dinner out, my fear that he was a psychopath. When I opened my eyes for the first time in months, he was there. Joy filled his features, not guilt, joy that I had returned to the living.

Opening my eyes to his image, I recalled the love, the tenderness, the tears. My thumb moved to the call icon, hovered there a moment, then touched it lightly.

One ring and I chickened out and pressed the call end button. What was I doing? All those memories were fake, a silly comatose dream. He probably wasn't anything like the man I conjured in my fantasies. I couldn't talk to him. I couldn't forgive him. I couldn't love him. It had all just been a crazy dream.

I turned the phone off again and packed it into my bag. I could get my own phone now, so the next time I saw Rachel, I had decided to return this one to Cole. I didn't need *anything* from him… did I?

Avoiding Romantic Comedies and Dramas, I searched for something on TV to pass the time. My hospital phone surprised me in the middle of a thriller, and I answered it without thinking.

"Hello?"

"Andi?"

"Yes, who's this?" I knew it was Cole, but I didn't want him to know.

"It's Cole. I hear you're leaving the hospital tomorrow. Do you need any help with moving anything to your hotel room? Flowers or anything?" His voice sounded numb, distant, a little sad.

"Uhm… no, actually…" I glanced at the one floral arrangement left in the room. It had arrived today. "I had the nurses distribute the flowers to other patients in need of cheer, but thank you."

"Hm…" I could picture his head shaking with the

huff. "I knew you would do that. It's the kind of person you are. That's why I..." He stopped himself from saying the words.

"How could you possible know I would do that, Cole? For all you know, I threw them in the dumpster. You don't know me, Cole! You don't know *ME*." My face flushed with the reality of the statement. He didn't know me! And I didn't know him—not really, not at all.

"But I do know you. I've read all your work. I read your journals to you. And when I ran out of stories about your life, I shared my life with you. We do know each other, Andi. That's why you knew me when you woke up. That's why you knew Rachel. Please..." An excitement returned to his voice, a desperate need to keep me on the line, win me over. I could hear it.

"And all those words, all those stories, all that time, just jumbled up into a giant mess of a dream in which I couldn't decide whether you were my killer or my lover. Now I know why I thought you were trying to kill me! My god, Cole! This thing that you think we have between us is as much a fantasy as the crazy dreams I had while in a coma. This could never work! It could never happen!" My words failed to match the shaky desire in my voice and I hoped he didn't hear how much I really wanted to believe it could work. If he was anything in real life like he was in my dreams, then I wanted it... I wanted him. But he couldn't be the man I dreamed of. I didn't know who he was. I slammed the phone onto the cradle and fell back onto my pillow in tears.

* * *

My eyes were puffy and red when I looked into the mirror the next morning. I'd showered and prepared for my last day in the hospital, and now I patted cold water on the bags beneath my eyes trying to reduce the swelling. While I packed the hairbrush into the bag on the bed, the nurse entered the room. "Well! Somebody's ready to leave this place! I can't blame you."

"Don't take it personally. You've been an incredible day nurse. I just think it's time for me to fly now." I joked.

"Didn't sleep too well, huh?" She swiped her index fingers beneath her own eyes and raised her brows.

"No, I guess not. It's just an odd feeling, starting over completely from scratch. It's like the first day of school or something." I shrugged.

"Argh! I always hated the first day of school! I never slept the night before. What a memory!" She laughed. "Well, the PT doctor should be here in a few minutes. Once she signs off, you're good to go. There's a guy waiting in the lobby. He said he's your driver. You want me to send him back to take your things to the car?" She hung the chart outside the door again.

"Uhm… that would great actually! Thanks!" I

nodded.

"What a lovely bouquet of flowers!" She spied them as she reached for the door handle.

I quickly moved to the arrangement and handed them to her, "Here! Take them. You've been so awesome to me, and I won't have room for them at the hotel."

"Are you sure?" She sniffed the flowers and peered through them at me.

"Yes, I am. I mean, the hotel room is going to have to serve as an office space as well, so the less interferences with living and working there are the better," I nodded.

"Thank you so much!" She pulled the card free and returned it to me, "You might want this, though."

Would I?

The car was packed by the time the nurse wheeled me down to the first floor exit. The driver opened the backseat door just as we approached. His tall slender frame stood patiently on the other side of the door as I stood from the wheel chair and turned to hug the nurse whom I'd felt I'd known for a lifetime. After situating myself in the back seat, the driver shut the door and walked briskly around the front of the vehicle to the driver's seat.

The short ride to the hotel didn't provide time for conversation making the drive feel like hours. I watched buildings, trees, and people pass by the window as the car moved easily through traffic up the main avenue through town.

A bellhop met us at the front entrance to the historic hotel and helped me to the room with my bags. I felt horrible that I didn't have a tip, but he assured me it wasn't a problem. The first thing I needed to do was find an ATM to get some cash so this wouldn't happen, again.

Once the door closed behind the bellhop, I leaned into it and took a look at my home for the next... however many days. I would need to find an apartment soon. Living in this room, though it was luxurious compared to the hospital, would drive me insane.

I unpacked my bags into the closet and the small dresser under the television, picking up the remote then setting it back down. Instead, I went to the window and opened the curtains to chase back dark corners. The sidewalks were bustling for a Monday and I watched people enter and exit shops and restaurants below. Suddenly, taking a walk down that sidewalk felt like a good idea. It was a small town and I remember how I'd always felt safe here. I found some jeans and a nice pullover shirt and placed them on the bed. I laid my tennis shoes and socks next to the bed as well. Digging through the only bag I hadn't unpacked, I found my hairbrush and hair tie to pull my hair into a messy bun. I never cared for a ponytail swinging back and forth across my back. I tucked my phone wallet and room key into the back pocket on my jeans and started out the door.

* * *

Out on the sidewalk, I felt alive for the first time in months, like a regular member of society. I was so grateful to be free of the hospital that I smiled and spoke to everyone I passed on the sidewalk. A positive feeling spread across my chest as I noticed all the little things I'd missed for months: birds flying out from under eves or out of trees, the smell of bakeries, flowers blooming in whisky barrel planters in front of shops, the smell of coffee brewing inside shops, the way strangers lit up when you greeted them with a smile, the laughter of small children in the park, the scent of fresh cut grass. It was a new beginning.

I sat in the park for a while and watched people, then I stopped for coffee and a pastry on my way back to the hotel.

* * *

When I returned, there was a letter on the floor as I opened the door and the largest bouquet of flowers I'd ever received sitting on the table inside my room. I was pretty sure who sent them without opening the card on the bouquet, so I opened the letter instead.

It was brief. Cole had said so much in a few words. I was in too good of a mood not to forgive him. It was the past. I'd been given a second chance at life and I wouldn't allow it to be ruined by anger or any other residual negative feelings. I pulled the card free and read the inside. Smiling, I inhaled deeply the scent of the roses. They were beautiful. Sitting at the small table in my room, I reached for the cell phone on the night stand. I took a picture of the flowers and texted it to Cole with a Thank You beneath the image.

It was an accident… after all. A stupid accident that changed my life, but in reality, my life had been changing long before that mild tap on my bike tire. As I sat staring out the window, I felt gratitude that Matt had left me in the hospital when he did, that I hadn't awakened and returned to the abuse the doctor discovered had existed before the accident. If not for that very minor accident due in part to my flight response and lack of attention to vehicles near me, Matt and I might have married, had children, and then he might have left later in our marriage anyway, or worse, I might not have survived. What then? I was beginning to see the silver lining as I watched the ebb and flow of traffic below me. If it hadn't been for the accident—

Cole had sat by my side, without knowing me, every day while I recuperated. Could he have developed real feelings for me during that time just from reading my journals? It seemed impossible. But then, anything was possible.

The thought of my journals sent me in search of paper. My box of journals lay in the closet floor, so I opened the lid to find an empty one on top the stack. A sticky note was attached, and I didn't have to read it to know who put it there. Still, I read the note.

> *In case you want to catch up on life.*
> *Cole*

Only a writer would know the joy that simple note brought me. A package of pens lay next to the journal and I opened it to remove a blue pen.

The warm sunshine filled my room as I wrote in the journal. I'd always loved the feel of a pen and paper to write personal thoughts, though I'd used a computer to write articles. My laptop, courtesy of the magazine's courier delivery, lay on the table opposite the notebook, but I didn't feel like using it. Hours later when I broke from writing my story, my stomach growled and I realized I hadn't eaten for several hours. I called room service to have something delivered and checked the mini fridge for a drink. It was fully stocked. Grabbing a small bottle of water, I returned to the table and my journal to continue writing. At this rate, I would need to transfer to my computer at some point as the words flowed so freely from thought to pen. I found it difficult to stop writing when room service arrived, announced by a light knock on the door

"One second!" I called out in answer as I finished a sentence.

Famished, I pulled the door open to a cart that immediately filled the room with glorious scents of a perfectly cooked burger and fries, "Thank you so much!" I looked up from the spread into the face of the…

Cole.

He smiled that dreamy, sexy, warm smile he had shared with me so many times in my lost state of mind, the smile I'd never really seen on his face until now. His eyes lit with desire and something else…

Returning his smile, I widened the path through the door and moved aside, bowing my head as he pushed the cart through.

"I hope you don't mind that I added a duplicate to your order." He moved the cart to the table and turned to look at me.

"I don't mind, but the person paying for the room might. You see, I'm only staying here interim. My benefactor might not like that you added a meal." I shrugged.

"Hmm… I'm sure I can handle him. There's a note here for you. I guess it's from the chef? I don't know." He handed me the white envelope emblazoned with hotel name and address. "Maybe it's a bill," he shrugged. The envelope was open.

"Did you open it to look? Because, the chef and I, we have this thing…" I played along.

"Is that right?" He took a step closer to me.

I pulled the paper free to open it.

"Before you read it, tell me you forgive me," Cole pinched one corner of the folded paper together before my thumb could flip it open. That was the request that lit his eyes when I looked at him, the need for forgiveness.

"Oh, I see. We're back to that bossy attitude."

"Bossy?"

"Never mind. Turns out it was all a dream, a very realistic dream." I smiled into his worried eyes, "Yes, I forgive you. It was an accident." I shrugged. "It could have happened to anyone. I wasn't paying attention. You weren't paying attention. And, the more I thought about it, the more I realized it was a blessing in disguise. But…" he removed his hold on the paper in my hand.

"Read it," he ordered.

"You really are incredibly bossy. You know that's going to be a problem for me. I'll never do what you say because I'm—"

"Bull headed? Yeah. Strong willed? Yes. Beautiful? Absolutely. Tender hearted? True. Loving? For certain. I could go on."

"You don't know me like you think you do," I contested.

"Oh, but, I do. You can't read everything a person wrote, everything about their life, without knowing that person. I know you well enough."

And I knew him. I knew him because he sat by bed

for eight months, four days and three hours reading me my stories, telling me his. The dreams I'd had during that dark time may have come from a lost mind, but they were as real as we were in that moment, facing each other with a desire so deep, a relationship so old, yet so new.

He reached out and unfolded the paper before me.

Smiling, I let my gaze fall to the paper in my hands.

BTW, I will always love you.

"I thought about sending you a text reply…" he started.

I was in his arms before he could finish his sentence.

He lowered his lips to mine as the light pressure from my hands at the nape of his neck drew his face toward mine. "Are you sure?" He whispered before our lips touched.

"Yes."

There were still unanswered questions, problems to resolve, life goals to achieve, mountains to overcome, but I didn't have to do it alone; I didn't have to live life alone, afraid, or troubled about where life would take me next.

Thank you for reading my novel, *By the Way...*

Would you do me a favor and post a review of this book on the site of purchase?

Also, would you share your review on my Facebook page?

https://www.facebook.com/AuthorPGShriver

Reviews are greatly appreciated by authors and readers alike. Thanks, again! Have a love filled day!

Born in California, and raised in Minnesota and Texas, P.G. spent her early years writing poetry and winning poetry contests, while escaping the drama of childhood by reading great books.

P.G. sought an education at the University of Texas, where English, literature, and Education became interests. During the entire process of earning a BA and M. Ed writing never stopped and getting published became a greater goal.

P.G. graduated college and began a career in education. She is currently retired from teaching after two rear end car accidents rendered her physically, mentally, and emotionally incapable of handling the stress and demands associated with her profession.

By the Way is P.G.'s first romantic thriller in her new *Blue Stone Ranch Romance* series which is dedicated to breaking the silence and the circle of abuse in families.